"I thought we were going to keep this outing more upbeat," Jacob said.

"This place does carry a lot of happy memories," Hollie replied.

"Like camping under the stars."

"Skinny-dipping under the waterfall." The words fell out of her mouth before she could think. She looked away quickly.

She missed him, she acknowledged to herself. For so many weeks, she'd shoved aside that thought, fearing she couldn't get through this if she let herself remember any of the good times together. But was that fair to their past?

He skimmed a knuckle down her arm. "We decompressed here more than once."

Once her pulse steadied, she risked a glance back at him and admitted, "The best anniversary gift you ever gave me was widening the path to get here."

His throat moved in a slow, emotional bob. "I'd have paved the entire thing if it could have..."

"I know." She rested a hand over his. Too often she got so wrapped up in her pain that she lost sight of his.

But she knew he'd gone through hell, too. Who else would ever understand so well? Tenderness welled up inside her.

Before she could think or reason, she angled forward and pressed her mouth to his.

Dear Reader,

As I'm the mother of a large family and now a grandmother of an even larger family, vacations prove to be a challenge. How do we find a location with something to offer for each person? What about accommodations for holidays? For different seasons? Pilates? Hobbies? As well as being animal-friendly! Well, it's been a delight to create that one-size-fits-all vacation getaway in my Top Dog Dude Ranch series.

Research is especially fun as I explore everything from goat yoga to barn dances. And in my research, I've also noticed that many dude ranches offer wedding packages with different themes. Given that the hero and heroine for *Last Chance on Moonlight Ridge*, Jacob and Hollie O'Brien, are on the brink of divorce, viewing all those weddings at their ranch will present a special challenge, forcing them to face the ghosts in their past.

Thank you for picking up the latest installment of my Top Dog Dude Ranch series. I look forward to hearing what you think of Hollie and Jacob's journey—and hearing which of the wedding themes was your favorite!

Cheers,

Catherine Mann

CatherineMann.com

PS: Be on the lookout for more novels in my Top Dog Dude Ranch series, coming soon from Harlequin Special Edition!

Last Chance on Moonlight Ridge

CATHERINE MANN

HARLEQUIN
SPECIAL
EDITION

Recycling programs
for this product may
not exist in your area.

ISBN-13: 978-1-335-40849-5

Last Chance on Moonlight Ridge

Harlequin Enterprises ULC
22 Adelaide St. West, 41st Floor
Toronto, Ontario M5H 4E3, Canada
www.Harlequin.com

Printed in U.S.A.

USA TODAY bestselling author **Catherine Mann** has won numerous awards for her novels, including both a prestigious RITA® Award and an *RT Book Reviews* Reviewers' Choice Award. After years of moving around the country bringing up four children, Catherine has settled in her home state of South Carolina, where she's active in animal rescue. For more information, visit her website, catherinemann.com.

Books by Catherine Mann

Harlequin Special Edition

Top Dog Dude Ranch

Last Chance on Moonlight Ridge
Last-Chance Marriage Rescue
The Cowboy's Christmas Retreat

Harlequin Desire

Alaskan Oil Barons

The Baby Claim
The Double Deal
The Love Child
The Twin Birthright
The Second Chance
The Rancher's Seduction
The Billionaire Renegade
The Secret Twin

Texas Cattleman's Club: Houston

Hot Holiday Rancher

Visit the Author Profile page
at Harlequin.com for more titles.

To my mother and father, who taught me the importance and joy of having dogs, cats, rabbits, fish and even ducks as a part of the family.

Chapter One

Her wedding dress still fit.

The marriage, however?

It was exploding at the seams.

Hollie O'Brien smoothed her hands down the fitted lace gown, tiny seed pearls beading under her fingertips just as they'd done two decades ago. Even though she hadn't been able to do up the buttons in back just now, the satin-and-lace creation felt the same against her skin, molding to her figure without being too snug.

Thank goodness it wasn't too small, since she'd put off pulling it from the back of her closet until the very last minute. Avoiding memories?

Absolutely.

But now, time was up, and she had to face all this gown represented—all that she'd lost. She spun in front of the antique full-length mirror, her bedroom suite behind her in a rustic chic wash of blue velvet brocade and dark pine walls.

She'd put such care in choosing the dress back then, full of hope, confident that she and Jacob could withstand any storms life sent their way. She'd been naive—and so very wrong.

This definitely wasn't the way she'd expected to celebrate her twentieth—the china—anniversary. Maybe that porcelain was prophetic, in some way, about the fragile nature of happiness. She and Jacob had exhausted every option—every alteration, so to speak—in hopes of salvaging their fractured union.

How ironic that they had built a thriving business focused on mending broken hearts and damaged relationships. Their Top Dog Dude Ranch perched in the Great Smoky Mountains was a success—and yet none of that reputed healing magic had shimmered over onto them.

At least she didn't have to hang on much longer. She just had to make it through the next two weeks with her sanity intact. Their dude ranch was featuring a massive spring weddings event. Nonstop weddings for the next fourteen days.

What pure torture, especially now.

When they'd planned this event a year ago, it had seemed like a brilliant idea to combine their anniversary month with a spring weddings theme. As part of the promotion, she'd gotten roped into putting on her gown for a photo shoot to be featured alongside images from their original ceremony.

But the positive press from the event was crucial for drumming up business. They needed the extra cash now more than ever. The expansion to a second Tennessee locale would give them each a place to live and autonomy in running their own division of the business. Otherwise, they would have to sell off the whole enterprise and split the proceeds once their divorce was final.

Hitching up the hem, she bunched lace in her hands, her buff-colored cowgirl boots tapping on the hardwood floor as she turned. She'd dreamed of passing the gown on to a daughter one day.

Even thinking of children brought a hitch to her throat and an ache all the way to her soul over so many losses. Miscarriages. Infertility. Her body had failed her.

Dropping on the end of her four-poster canopy bed, she sagged back, fingertips tracing the patterns in the creamy tapestry throw blanket like a talisman. Rumor had it the bed came from an old saloon. She prided herself on decorating the ranch with authenticity, the cabins with a Western vibe. She'd thrown herself into the business to fill empty hours.

To distract her thoughts from the grief that had hovered at the edges of her marriage for so long.

Her gray tabby leaped from the floor, to the navy paisley cushion, then settled onto her lap, purring. She threaded her fingers though the cat's fur, medium length and plush rather than the typical shorter tabby coat. Pippa purred louder, pressing closer. Most people didn't know a cat's purr matched a hertz level that supposedly increased bone density and healing. She'd told ranch attendees that this was just one of the beauties of nature they utilized to help ranch guests. It was a miracle and science all wrapped up together. How many times had she preached that people who trusted the animal-assisted pack-tivities would feel the Top Dog healing boost?

Right now, she doubted that even a litter of kittens could mend her broken heart. Pippa mewed, nestling further into her lap as if to comfort Hollie's unspoken pain. Petting under her cat's chin, she took a deep breath. Then another.

She faced such a lonely future without her

husband, without even her child. They'd finally embraced hope through adoption, welcoming a precious baby boy into their lives, only to have the birth mother change her mind and take the child back.

That had been the true beginning of the end for them. The blow had been fierce when, as a couple, they had already given all they had left inside. She hugged Pippa closer, only to realize she'd gotten fur on her dress, kitty hair dark against the white satin and stubbornly wrapped around seed pearls.

Standing, she eased Pippa to the floor and searched for the lint roller. A bark outside the bedroom door gave her only a second to react before a border collie Lab mix puppy bolted inside.

"Bandit, settle," she called.

The pup ignored her, bounding and barking. Close on his heels, her Scottish terrier—Scottie—trotted, quietly, but radiating energy with each speedy wag of his stubby tail.

Pippa hissed, hair standing up along her spine. Uh-oh.

The feline darted under the bed in a blur of mottled fur. Bandit took chase. Scottie shot beneath the puppy, taking the lead.

Squealing, Hollie stumbled out of the way. "Pippa, Bandit, Scottie, please..."

She searched for the best way to corral them without tripping or diving onto her knees after them. The photo shoot would be ruined if she showed up in a torn and muddy gown, her hair sticking out every which way.

Grabbing the bedpost with one hand, she clapped the other to her chest to anchor her dress in place. Her booted feet tangled in the hem. She heard a rip and cringed, struggling to loosen her hold to save the gown that had suddenly become more precious than she would have admitted an hour ago.

Satin slithered from her grip, the fabric pooling at her feet. A gasp behind her sent her gaze flying up to the mirror again.

Her gaze met the reflection of—her husband.

Jacob O'Brien braced a hand against the door frame, his world rocked by the sight of his gorgeous wife, a wife he hadn't held or seen naked in months. Although technically, she wasn't naked, but close enough to make his blood sizzle.

Hollie stood with her wedding gown around her ankles, her wide blue eyes appearing every bit as stunned as he felt. Her dark brown hair tumbled over her shoulders in waves. The white satin of her strapless bra cupped her breasts, making his hands itch to sweep it away and take her to the bed, to their bed.

His mind scrolled back to the first time he'd seen her in the gown and when he'd peeled it from her that night on their honeymoon cruise. Their marriage had seen struggles, but they'd always connected on a physical level—until their son had been taken back by his birth mother.

Just the thought sent a stab of pain clean through him, echoed by scrolling memories of JJ's cherub cheeks and baby laugh. His eyes shifted to the place by their bed where JJ's basinet had rested.

A movement just past that too empty space shifted his attention back to the present.

The cat shot from under the four-poster bed, reminding him that he didn't want to risk anyone else seeing Hollie half-clothed. He closed the door quickly, throwing the bolt. Even though their quarters were private, that didn't preclude someone from the ranch staff searching for them. The day had turned into utter chaos—in more ways than one.

Jacob strode deeper into the room, kneeling to scoop her dress upward. Rising, he met her halfway as she bent forward at the same time. Their eyes met, so close he could see her pupils widening with awareness.

He needed distance.

He wanted his wife.

And there wasn't a chance he would get either.

Hollie took her dress from his fists, the brush of her touch electric, the lilac scent of her heady. His mouth watered for a taste of her.

Hitching the dress back up, she inspected every inch for damage as she pulled it in place again. A tiny tear showed along the hem. "I should have locked the door."

"At least the photographer wasn't with me." A dry smile kicked across his mouth. "Although I wouldn't mind having a few boudoir photos of you, for old time's sake."

"Not funny." She waved him away. "Go tell the photographer I'll be there as soon as I can get dressed. At least the rip is small and only in the hem."

Watching her struggle to reach behind herself, he finally said, "Do you, uh, need help?"

"Actually, yes. With the buttons." She sighed in exasperation. "I didn't think this through, and I can't reach them. How much longer do I have?"

"The photographer's ready to roll. There's not time for me to do anything more than help you." He steeled his resolve, cupped her shoulders and turned her around.

She swept aside her flowing brown hair, sun

through the part in the curtains shimmering on the barest hint of auburn. He barely succeeded in biting back a groan of appreciation at the thin strip of flesh leading from the nape of her neck to the top of her sweet bottom.

"Jacob?" She looked over her shoulder, her blue eyes wide.

Clearing his throat, he began fastening the tiny pearl buttons. Heaven help him, there were so very many of them, and as much as he wanted to take his time, that wasn't an option. So he just soaked up the feel of her velvety skin under his knuckles as he made fast work of closing the gap. "Who took care of this the first time?"

"My mother." Her voice washed over him, soft and musical. "She did my makeup and even arranged the flowers. She had such a gift."

"I'm sorry she can't be here to help you now— during this transition, I mean." He hated to think of her alone.

He also hated to think of her moving on with another man.

"It's not like our split is a surprise, Jacob. I've had time to adjust. It's the waiting that's the hardest part right now."

Time to adjust? How could she be so glib about their life being torn apart? Her calm rationale cut right through him—and pissed him off. He fastened the last button. "There. All set."

"Thank you." She let her hair slide back into place, the strands slithering over his hand.

"You look…gorgeous."

"That's kind of you to say, but not needed." She pivoted to face him again, her eyes full of so much awareness, pain…memories.

All that raw emotion, feelings echoing inside him, threatened to drive him to his knees. "Hollie, babe—"

Shaking her head, she flattened a hand on his chest. "I guess we should get moving if we want to finish up before the first of the wedding couples arrive. I'll just staple the hem. No one will notice."

"Oh, man." He thumped himself on the head. "I came here to tell you about the change in scheduling."

"What change?" She frowned as she hastily put on dangly pearl earrings.

"The vans for the kiddie camp are running ahead of time. They'll be here an hour early." Thank goodness his efficient wife would have seen that details were ready far ahead of time. He didn't know how he would manage without her— in so many ways.

"We need to get moving, then." She suddenly shifted into high gear, gathering her leather work-bag full with her tablet and notes. She fished out a stapler, and with two quick clicks, the rip disappeared. She hastily threw in a makeup bag and a brush. "That's going to cut it close with getting the photo shoot complete and checking in the wedding couples and then changing back into the Western gear, but we should be able to pull it off before the kids arrive."

"Um, the bus with the first two wedding parties is stuck on the road because a bear is blocking the way."

"A bear?" Her face flooded with pure panic. "Jacob, that means all those kids will be arriving at the same time as the wedding parties. It's going to be chaos."

Chaos? Yep. He'd thought the same thing at the idea of a bear in the road. It was like even the animals were conspiring against them.

He just needed to get through the next two weeks. Then he could hunker down and recover. Not for the first time, he wished he would be the one moving to the new locale. All the memories of Hollie—of their son—would be a specter he wasn't sure how he would navigate.

"Here comes the bride." From the pond's dock, the photographer pivoted, silk scarf on his shoulder billowing behind him into the breeze.

Hollie picked her way down the wooded trail, her lace dress bunched in her hands. Her assistant held the train off the ground in a pseudo bridesmaid style as they made their way to the promo shoot. Spring caressed the branches of the trees reaching over the water, a splash of light greens and flower buds swaying in the cool mountain air. Jacob would be joining her as soon as he changed into his "groom's" gear for the photography session.

At least they were out of the house, with the buffer of other people—and her dress wasn't down around her ankles.

Her heart still hammered double time in her chest, her skin clinging to the memory of his touch along her back as he buttoned her gown. She needed to get her head out of the past, ditch all the memories of their wedding, their marriage, and focus on nailing this photo shoot.

The dock provided a prime spot to showcase the ranch, the mountains and valleys, so lush right now after the saturation of hefty winter storms. A couple paddled a lazy canoe in the distance, adding to the idyllic tableau. The waters narrowed into a stream that trickled over the rocks, and it followed for a mile, it connected to the hot springs inside Sulis Cave.

A breeze blew through, the mountain air cool even with approaching summer. She rubbed her arms against the chill.

"Do you want my jacket?" her assistant offered as they closed in on the photographer and reporter.

Ashlynn had joined their team last fall to help during the transition. A dear friend and foster sister of the co-owner of the new branch outside of Nashville, Ashlynn was a perfect fit for their Top Dog family. She floated back and forth between the two Tennessee locations for now, and would settle with Hollie at the new branch once the transition was complete for her to leave Moonlight Ridge.

Home.

"I'm good for now," she said, swallowing down a lump and waving to the photographer in the distance as he walked around, checking lighting. "Thank you, Ashlynn."

"I came prepared. I have a Top Dog windbreaker in my bag." She held up a boho bag, opening it to reveal not only an extra jacket, but also a makeup bag, brush, and hair spray, for the photo shoot, no doubt. Ashlynn was a gem.

"If you're sure. I wouldn't mind draping one over my shoulders." She plucked out the windbreaker with the Top Dog logo. "Hopefully we'll get started soon. It's going to be a zoo around here having two buses arrive at the same time."

If it had been another wedding party showing up ahead of schedule, that would have been more manageable, since the welcome packet and activities were the same. But the vans with the children required a whole different type of welcome.

On the plus side, maybe the photographer would feature the children, too. Two dozen kids in the foster care system had been gifted with scholarships for a vacation at the ranch. One of the wedding guests had come up with the idea to make that his gift to a bride and groom. A truly lovely sentiment from a philanthropist, and one Ashlynn had taken a special interest in overseeing, given her own experience in foster care. Photo releases had been obtained for each child, with the hope of encouraging people to foster.

The whinny from a horse had Hollie looking over her shoulder. Jacob strode down the path, surefooted, leading Nutmeg—a blood bay Thoroughbred they had helped rescue and rehab from a neglect situation. Delicate sprigs of jasmine were threaded throughout the horse's reddish-brown mane. Nutmeg's neck arched majestically, making him look like something from a fairy-tale book. Her husband, decked out in wedding finery for the photo shoot, took her breath away every bit as much now as he had when they first married. He wore a black tuxedo with a bolo tie, a Stetson and cowboy boots. He was her every fantasy wrapped up in muscles and determination, honor and charm.

Except fantasies often didn't hold up to the harsh light of reality. He'd been supportive during the fertility treatments and cancer battle, but she'd seen the strain on him. Not that he shared his worries and fears with her.

She pulled her attention back to the photographer. He was new to the paper, but she'd met him last week to determine the schedule and show him to the cabin they'd designated for his use to save time driving to the ranch every day. "Thank you for being a part of our spring weddings event, Mr. Clark. Where would you like us to stand?"

"Call me Milo. Please." The photographer tugged on his graying beard, eyeing the landscape, his camera dangling around his neck. "I was thinking we could start out there on the little bridge over the stream. Will it hold up with the horse?"

Jacob stroked a hand along Nutmeg's muzzle. "Absolutely. Everything here is built to code. We've even hosted an entire dinner party on that bridge."

Milo waved them on. "Lead the way. I can get photos as we walk as well. How about hitch up the train and clasp hands with your husband. Mr. O'Brien, you lead the horse and pretend I'm just a regular guest who's taking a tour. Forget about the camera."

Easier said than done.

Hollie shrugged off the jacket and passed it to Ashlynn before linking fingers with Jacob, his touch warm and familiar. His warm brown gaze held her as firmly as his hand. Authentic? Or for the camera?

There'd been a time when this was so easy and natural for them. Now it was all just staged for business. The sound of the camera clicking serenaded them from behind, capturing images she knew would break her heart when she viewed them later.

Ashlynn walked alongside them, hitching her cavernous boho bag onto her shoulder. She tugged free strands of black curls that snagged under the strap before flashing the photographer a curious smile. "Milo, how much do you know about the history of Moonlight Ridge? It's got quite a special legend."

"I'm new around here," the photographer answered, sweeping to the side for more photos. "Fill me in on the details so I can include it in our feature."

"Well," Hollie said, "there is a cave with hot springs. We have hours it's open for any patrons, like a pool. Our guests can also schedule time slots to indulge as a family, couple, or private party. One of the bridesmaids has reserved it for a bachelorette party."

"What a unique idea." The photographer jogged ahead, huffing, then knelt for another shot.

Hollie tried to ignore how she and her husband's steps had synched up, a habit of two decades together, instinctive. "We have another bridal party indulging in a spa day. Lonnie and Patsy—our massage therapists—have worked with us from the start and assist with many of our events. They're also renewing their vows."

"Mr. O'Brien, could you put your arm around your wife's waist? Is the spa day at the springs?"

Her thoughts scattered at the strength of his arm, the spicy scent of his aftershave.

"The spa day can be at the springs." Jacob picked up the conversational slack before the silence grew too noticeable. "But the massage therapists can travel to different locations at the ranch. The hot springs are called also called Sulis

Springs. It's reputed that magic carried from the Old World still lives with nearby animals."

"Tell me some more about that." Milo gestured for her to rest her head on Jacob's shoulder as they neared the bridge over the creek.

Had Jacob kissed her on top of the head? Instinctively? Or for show? Either way, she tingled all the way to the roots of her hair.

"Once upon a time," Jacob said, his deep breath rustling her hair, "when my ancestors were settling into this area from Scotland and Ireland, they followed a doe to the cave opening. It wasn't just any old doe, though."

Hollie slid into their routine easily, taking comfort in the familiarity of it. Had she used the rituals to avoid real connection before now? Very likely. "She was the Queen of the Forest, and she glowed like starlight."

"My ancestors knew the type of animal well." Jacob stopped at the foot of the bridge, bringing her hand to his chest as the camera snapped away. "They used to roam Scotland and lead wayward souls to safe places and healing waters that offered respite and a way to connect. My ancestors met all sorts of challenges in getting settled into this region. They wanted to give up on the land—even on each other. But legend has it, when they were at the end of their rope, they followed the Queen of the Forest to the cave mouth."

Milo eased down toward the creek, using the lower angle to aim the lens up at them. "Keep going. This is all good stuff."

"There was a lost pup in the cave whimpering." Her mind echoed with the memory of her child's cries, a sound that still tortured her dreams as she wondered if he wept for her, wondering why she wasn't there to comfort him. "They searched and searched. Just when they'd given up hope, they found the scruffy little creature shivering, its paw caught between some rocks. They worked it free— but the real miracle is that the puppy didn't even growl or bite during the process."

Jacob's brown eyes darkened, as if he sensed her thoughts. "So, while they waited for a pot of coffee to brew over the fire, they cleaned up the young pup. As they rinsed the puppy, their bond was renewed. Healed. They found a way to work with the land, with each other."

Silence stretched, a woodpecker's rhythm conspicuously loud, but she had nothing to offer up. Her mouth had gone dry. Jacob simply stared back, his eyes awash with pain he never acknowledged.

Ashlynn cleared her throat. "It's magic," she interjected. "Much like how our hot springs have healed and gathered people to Moonlight Ridge for over a hundred years. We have a reputation for bringing people together because of it."

Together?

She felt like a total fraud, peddling snake oil. No matter how many couples and families she saw healed after their time at the ranch, it felt hollow with her own life falling apart. Her hands went cold, a chill that iced all the way to her soul.

Just as she started to angle away, to call an end to this torture, the photographer's voice cut through.

"Mr. O'Brien," Milo announced, "you may kiss your bride."

Chapter Two

The edict from the photographer knocked around in Jacob's brain, rolling him back to twenty years ago when he'd held Hollie in his arms and called her his bride. How could she feel so familiar and such a stranger all at once? Time and heartbreak had changed them, and there was nothing left but to forge ahead.

"It's just a kiss," he said softly, as much for his own sake as for Hollie's. But it had never been just a kiss with her—he couldn't imagine a time when he would be unaffected by having her close.

"For the camera," she whispered, blue eyes sparkling like the morning sky. Her fingers moved restlessly against his lapel.

"For the ranch."

Nutmeg nudged him on the shoulder, a velvety nose reminder to get on with it. An almost inaudible nicker from his horse pushed him to action.

Jacob skimmed his mouth over hers, once, twice, holding. He wanted to stay like this, to extend the moment revisiting the past. Was it his imagination or had she swayed into him? Her tongue brushed against his, just a flutter, a taste of her favorite tea and honey she drank at breakfast.

Hope rose in his chest for the briefest moment as twenty years ago pressed visions into his mind's eye. He knew this pose well—Hollie's long hair spilling down her back, his hand braced along her waist. Twenty years ago, their wedding photographer had captured them in this exact position. And every day, Jacob had glanced at a canvas print of that image that had hung in the bedroom. It was so damn easy to get lost in those memories, in the promises and dreams from that moment.

Except this wasn't the past. She didn't want him or their marriage or their life together anymore, not since JJ had been ripped from their lives. When he'd urged for one last try to adopt, she'd shut him down cold, stating she would never risk that pain again.

Not long after, she'd asked him for a divorce.

She'd told him he deserved the family she no longer felt able to give him. He stopped trying to convince her otherwise. After so many years of them both struggling to repair their marriage after relentless blows from fate, he was just worn out and ready to throw in the towel.

These next two weeks would be their swan song. So he'd better get to work on making it memorable for them both, starting with this kiss. She would no doubt push him away soon if he didn't step back. Instead, he gave the photographer one last tableau. He dipped Hollie back into an old-fashioned, romantic kiss, photo worthy. His mouth on hers, he drew in her scent. Her breathy sigh tendriled into him.

Before she could shake off the dazed look in her eyes or protest, he swept her onto her feet again.

Milo wolf-whistled. "Now, that's the money shot. I can already see it as the lead photo in our feature. The readers are going to eat this up."

Unease gnawed at Jacob's gut as he thought of the fallout that could come once those same readers realized their marriage was a sham. They'd hoped to use the excuse of the ranch expansion to explain Hollie's absence. But if they started divorce proceedings, surely that would leak out into their close-knit community of Moonlight Ridge.

A rogue idea hit him.

What if he used these next two weeks to convince Hollie not to file for divorce? Even if she still moved to the new location, staying married would certainly make things easier from a business perspective. And he sure didn't want to venture into wedded bliss with anyone ever again.

The notion gained momentum in his mind—a marriage of convenience with his own wife.

"Jacob?" Hollie tugged on his bolo tie. "Are you in there? Look."

She pointed toward the distant mountain road where a bus peeked through the trees, winding its way to the lodge. He bit down a curse, then exhaled hard. Couldn't anyone stick to a schedule today?

As if on cue, his cell phone chimed with messages, then Hollie's, then Ashlynn's, weaving into a techno symphony of urgency.

"Ashlynn, once Milo packs up, could you escort our photographer friend back up the to the lodge? We'll meet you there. It'll be quicker if we ride." He tossed the truck keys to Ashlynn. Without waiting for the answer, he swung up onto his horse and settled into the saddle. "But first, Mr. Clark, I think you're going to want to snag a few photos of this."

Jacob extended an arm to Hollie, inviting her to join him on Nutmeg.

Hollie could have sworn her boots grew roots.

As she stared at her husband's outstretched arm, she knew she should just clasp it and swing up behind him as she'd done countless times in the past. But with that kiss still shimmering through her, the thought of sharing a horseback ride with him, pressing against him, inhaling his scent, hearing his heartbeat, was just too much.

Her body, her senses were on overload.

She clenched her fists, manicured fingertips digging into the soft parts of her palms. The smile she'd conjured for the images fell away. Lips tightened now into a thin line, her cheeks as tense as her chest. Air suddenly seemed in short supply.

"Hollie..." Jacob's deep voice swept over her like amber whiskey to the senses. "Are you worried about messing up your hair? I promise not to ride too fast."

How like Jacob to step in with an excuse that would save face in front of the photographer. He was always quick on his feet like that, whereas she was full of emotion driving the train of her thoughts and actions.

How much longer would they have to pretend for the world? She was weary with the subterfuge.

Only two more weeks, she reminded herself. Two more weeks until she could move on without constant reminders of her failures poking the embers of her pain into a flame.

Mouth quirking up into a pamphlet-ready grin, she smoothed her dress and tried to ignore the scratch of the staples in the hem. Sweat had begun to bead on her palms. A result of the stress mounting as the photographer documented the lies her heart could no longer bear to believe.

She shot out her hand, clasped Jacob's, and shut down thoughts of that warm calloused touch stroking her body. Jacob's brown eyes always had a steadying effect on her. Or they had. Right now, as she mounted the horse, those eyes felt like daggers into her heart. Reminders of a future that hadn't come to pass but had crumpled and yellowed like land in a drought.

In an instant, Ashlynn approached Nutmeg's left side. Her hands worked to fix the bunched fabric of her wedding dress and ease a staple out of sight. Ashlyn's eye for detail was impeccable. Though the dress was hitched mid-thigh, Ashlynn had arranged the drape so the fabric transformed from compressed mess to a stylish short gown.

"And bam. You look like a fairy tale now." Ashlynn's caramel eyes lit up as she surveyed her handiwork. Ashlynn waved at Jacob, signaling that they were ready to depart.

Hollie's arms slid around Jacob's thick, muscled torso. Her feet dangled as she sought stability for the ride. The irony of seeking stability from her soon-to-be-ex-husband was not lost on her. If anything, that knowledge sent her stomach into an impressive combination of twists, knots and leaps that would have taught even a master acrobat a thing or two.

Jacob drew in a deep breath, exhaling a clicking noise that caught Nutmeg's attention. The horse spiritedly took a step forward. Hooves knocked against the gravel path, stirring stones as they moved toward the lodge.

A slight dip in the path jostled Hollie forward and against Jacob. Enticingly so.

A year ago, the dip in the road and Nutmeg's peppy gait wouldn't have disrupted her seat so severely. Admittedly, she was distracted. Her mind and body were fatigued from oceans of sadness and the beginning storm clouds of impending loss.

Jacob clasped a hand over hers on his chest to steady her. "I thought that went very well."

"Which part?" Had she really just curled her

fingers into his shirt? "The photos or when you had your tongue in my mouth?"

He laughed softly, the chuckle rumbling through him and into her. "Well, both, I guess."

"I won't deny that I enjoyed it. We've always had chemistry." In spades.

Except grief had stolen even that from them, any connection full of too much emotion and so very little of it good. They had both been worn down by tragedy. It lingered between them as a constant reminder of all they had lost.

Twenty years ago, when she and Jacob were newlyweds full of freshly pressed dreams and laughter, this path through the forest had been her favorite feature of the land. She loved this trail in all seasons, but especially spring. Light green leaves decorated the branches. White flowers on bushes lined their way like nature's guide. The cool mountain breeze carried scents of fresh rain, mulch, and wildflowers waking from sleep.

The horse stepped over a rotting log, and she wrapped her arms tighter around his waist. "We both are taking care of business. We are doing what's necessary to launch the new location so I have a place to live when we separate."

His muscles tensed against her. "I'm glad you'll have Ashlynn with you, Nina and Douglas, too.

Although with their help on that end, there's no need to hurry the transition."

Nina and Douglas Archer owned the dairy farm that was being converted into an outpost of the Top Dog Dude Ranch. If anything, Hollie and Jacob had taken their time with the move. But arguing with Jacob would accomplish nothing except stealing the pleasure from a ride together on a beautiful day.

"It seemed providential timing that they came here as guests in danger of losing their farm at just the time we needed to expand, like this was meant to be the next stage in our lives."

"I feel bad you're having to relocate, away from everything familiar. This is your home, too."

He always had been an honorable man. She would never forget the way he'd stood by her during her cancer battle, staying by her side, giving of himself even when she knew his heart was in shreds. He deserved happiness—he deserved a family.

At least there was an upside to moving far away from everything familiar. She wouldn't be surrounded by reminders of the past. The son she'd lost.

"It only makes sense that I be the one to relocate. This is your family's land. I don't want to take away your legacy."

Although, as she looked around her, she could see ways that it was her legacy now, too. Under her loving care, she'd overseen the integration of Top Dog Dude Ranch signs into the natural woods. She'd made and tended the flower beds around each of the signs and trail paw print markers back in the old days. As they plodded along the trail, she saw versions of herself in every tree's shadow. Today the trail seemed filled with all the dreams lost. A new start away from memories tucked behind every branch seemed far easier for her broken heart to manage.

Hollie gripped Jacob tighter than she needed to as they approached the lodge—an impressive structure where so many families had gathered and healed. Just not them. Her impulse to squeeze him tight in moments of despair was a muscle memory, one she had no idea how to unlearn. A deep breath through her nose anchored her for a moment, her hold unfurling as she looked at the legacy she and Jacob had created. The work of a lifetime flooded her vision.

The center part of the lodge had been the original homestead, with additions as they expanded their venture. Guest cabins dotted the wooded landscape behind. Bunkhouses sprawled for staff and larger parties or retreats. She remembered the plans that went into every new development, every landmark on the way to building the life of their dreams.

They'd built something beautiful with what they could control. It was what they couldn't control that had been the death knell of their lives together.

Jacob cleared his throat. His voice reverberated through his back, warming Hollie for a moment as cool spring wind gusted. "Nina and Douglas have been talking up what a hit your puppy bakery and ice-cream shop will be along with their whole dairy farm vibe."

Hollie glanced up and fixed his black Stetson, which the spring wind had nearly knocked clear off his head. "You don't have to make small talk with me."

A pause stretched. For three long heartbeats, Nutmeg's hooves churning dirt and the chatter of squirrels in the awakening treetops were the only sounds.

"I hate that it's awkward between us." His voice was low, deflated in a way that caused Hollie's own chest to ache. "The silence between us is unnatural."

She shoved the pain down. Hollie did her best

to forget the way his gaze on her body had excited her. "Because of the incident with my dress?"

His laugh rumbled low and soft in his chest again. "That certainly didn't help."

"So, how do we get through the next two weeks with our sanity intact?"

Resting his hand over hers, silently, he guided Nutmeg ever closer to the busy lodge teeming with movement. For a moment, she felt the magnetic pull of their bodies still strong, still aware.

He cleared his throat. "We need to stay very, very busy."

"What do you mean?"

"We're still married, and knowing that is tempting. Especially when we're bumping into each other half-dressed. If we don't find ways to stay occupied…"

The implication was clear. Hollie was glad he couldn't see her, because she could feel the heat blooming in her cheeks. But he was wrong. They couldn't just pretend when they were alone the way they did in public.

"In name only, Jacob. In name only." This moment in the woods—alone time with her almost ex-husband—was coming to a close. She did her best impression of the Celtic queens from the fairy tales she'd grown up reading about. Straightening her spine, lifting her chin, she looked to the buses and vans approaching the lodge. Hollie felt waves of sheer kinetic energy bubbling from the vehicles.

As the charter bus pulling up to the lodge, with the promise of a van full of kids arriving not too long after, she suspected staying busy wasn't going to be a problem.

Breathless, with barely seconds to spare, Jacob took his place to welcome their guests, Hollie next to him, sweeping her train to the side and smoothing her hair back in place. Still, she had a tousled bedroom look that, as far as he was concerned, stirred thoughts of a honeymoon and beat any salon updo to go with her wedding gown.

Not that there was time for a touch-up. Thank goodness for Ashlynn's organization as all was set up before the photo shoot as there hadn't even been time to change.

An old-fashioned wood wagon was parked in front of the lodge entrance, decorated with twinkling lights and fat bows in pretty spring colors. Bales of hay were set up like tables on either side, food on one. Hollie stood at the other hay bale with their puppy to say hello. Thank goodness puppy Bandit had settled down. Of course, all that love from guests was a big motivator in his good behavior.

Daylight was still burning strong—albeit low—in the sky. A bonfire had been lit in the firepit to chase away the late afternoon chill. In the winter, that same spot served as an ice-skating rink. Nutmeg was now being ridden by a stable hand slowly weaving through the gathering, circling a lasso overhead.

Once the last patron stepped off the bus, Jacob flicked on the microphone. "Greetings! I'm Jacob O'Brien, and this lovely lady is Hollie, my bride of twenty years. Welcome to Moonlight Ridge, Tennessee, home to the Top Dog Dude Ranch, renowned for family-friendly rustic retreats that heal broken hearts. Some say it's the majestic mountain vistas. Others vow there's magic in the hot springs. All agree, there's something special about the four-legged creatures at Top Dog Dude Ranch that give guests a 'new leash on love.'"

Hollie took a step forward, a smile as radiant as the Tennessee morning sun playing on her lips and lighting her eyes. At every greeting session, Jacob made sure his full attention stayed with the incoming guests and small crowds. Today was different. Spring sunshine soaked his bride, making her seem like an ethereal princess of the forest.

His breath caught in his throat, and his eyes stayed with Hollie while she spoke. An unrestrained smile rested easy on his lips for once.

Hollie gave a gentle wave, gesturing to the photographer who was breathlessly setting up with Ashlynn assisting. "Mr. Clark over here will be taking photos for our local paper and their national outlets. You'll have complimentary access to all the pictures he takes, even the ones he doesn't use in the feature."

Cheers rippled through the crowd.

The bearded photographer waved. "Call me Milo."

Hollie continued, "If you would like to participate in the photo features, each couple or family or wedding party is invited to step up to the arbor. Come say hello to me and my husband, and tell Milo a little about your romance, and he'll snap photos."

Hopefully quickly.

Jacob's attention returned to those assembled before him. He did his best to meet the gazes of each visitor as he spoke. "Meanwhile, if you're waiting—or if you prefer not to be photographed— feel free to mingle, enjoy the munchies. Our assistant will also be on hand with your welcome packets."

He gestured to a wagon that the band—comprised of Top Dog employees—was using as a stage. The sound system pulsed with the strains of a guitar, banjo and fiddle tuning for an instant before their homegrown band—Raise the Woof—launched into a country tune.

Hollie leaned toward the photographer. "The drummer—Briggs—is engaged to the fiddle player—Eleanor. They'll be getting married next week as well."

Milo's bushy eyebrows rose. "Well, I sure hope they're first up on the roster, or you may have a baby delivery in the middle of the service."

He took aim with the lens directed at the very pregnant violin player. With the music thrumming through the speakers, the gathered crowd came alive. Movement flowed to and from the snack bar, folks sliding out to the dance floor. Couples pressed into each other, getting lost in private gazes and swaying hips.

A young couple rushed up, looking ready to hike mountain trails.

"Hi, I'm Allegra, and we would love a photo before we go exploring." Her raven-black hair was gathered in a high ponytail. She gave a warm smile as she came to a halt in front of Jacob.

"And I'm Simon," her fiancé said. A water bottle peeked out the side of his green-and-brown backpack.

Allegra placed her hand in Simon's, giving it a quick squeeze. She covertly pointed at two older couples in hot debate over by the buffet. "Ignore our parents. They haven't stopped bickering since the day we got engaged. That's part of why we decided to do a destination wedding. Less planning means less opportunity for controversy."

Simon adjusted the aviator glasses on his head. A half laugh infused with desperation leaped from his mouth. "Or so we thought."

"Today—" Allegra's lips pressed tight for a moment before she shook her head, voice dropping lower "—they're fighting because our moms think their dresses look too much alike. Our dads are mad because they're sharing a cabin."

Hollie's shoulder brushed Jacob's. "We can adjust the cabin assignments for you. We want you and your guests to be happy."

While they wanted to accommodate all visitors, this party in particular needed some kid glove handling. One of Allegra's uncles was the individual who'd sponsored the scholarships for the children in the group home to attend the Top Dog Dude Ranch for a week. A thoughtful gift, even though it made for such a hectic schedule.

"No, please." Allegra hitched her backpack higher on her shoulders and hooked arms with Simon. "This is the way we want it. They have to learn to get along sometime. We might as well start out like we can hold out. So far, the only thing they've agreed upon is how much they hate the idea of an eco-adventure wedding theme."

Simon pulled on the sleeve of his orange plaid shirt. "When I showed them the photos of the cake decorated with the lovely greenery reminiscent of our favorite hiking trail, Dad called it a chia cake."

Milo chuckled from behind the lens. "I'll have to be sure to snap a photo of that."

So much hope radiated from them in their smiles for the camera and whispered confidences as they walked back to join their families. And even in the parents' arguing, there was a clear pride and excitement coming through. Jacob missed his folks since they'd moved out West, and Hollie's mom, too, since she'd passed away. Their world was narrowing.

He pulled his attention back to the task at hand. He didn't need Milo snagging pictures of him looking distracted, or worse yet, morose.

Maybe he should have taken the meditation practice the ranch offered. Or signed up for acting classes. He could have used some more tools for producing and maintaining a facade of bliss outwardly. No matter. He could do this. He had to do this.

An older couple approached, their fingers as entwined as the ancient oak trees in the center of his family's land.

"We're Constance and Thomas." She pressed a hand to her chest, green eyes sparking as her wispy brunette pixie cut bounced with every step they took. Her words tumbled as fast as the river over rocks in the valley. "This is the first marriage for both of us. I know it may seem silly at my age, but I'm going to have the full fairy-tale wedding, with a tiara and all the trappings."

Thomas tucked her close, excitement glinting in his eyes. "Whatever my princess wants. Connie deserves to be treated like royalty. She is the woman of my dreams, and I'm so glad she waited for me to find her."

They stepped to the side for their photos, pausing for a passionate kiss, then another, until Jacob ran a finger under his shirt collar. Hollie pressed her temple like she always did when she was holding back tears.

Yeah, this sucked, seeing so much love radiating off the couple, imagining themselves at their age. The future looked…lonely.

Next up.

Sigh. How many more?

He pressed out a smile to greet the newest couple, decked out in Western gear. The bride-to-be wore a pale pink boho dress with russet cowgirl boots. She threaded her pale fingers with her fiancé's ebony ones.

"I'm Kendric and this is Natalie, and we can't think of a better place for a country wedding." Kendric's voice sounded like summer storms, melodic and powerful.

Natalie flashed a camera-ready smile. "We can chat later, honey. I want to make sure we get lots of photos for our memory album." She smiled fast, her eyes already trekking to Milo. "Nice to meet you, Jacob and Hollie."

And as if to pour alcohol on a thousand paper cuts, a family stepped up next, a mom and dad with two young children, radiating the image of total happiness.

"Hello," the mother said. "We're Fiona and Jayden Rossi, and these are our two children." She gestured with so much pride to the young girl in braided pigtails and toddler boy showing off his light-up tennis shoes.

Jayden hooked a finger in the back of his son's T-shirt to keep the boy from falling off the step.

"We're celebrating our tenth anniversary by renewing our vows with our children as witnesses."

Before he could expand on their story, the toddler with a mop of blond curls squirmed out of his dad's hold and took off, his shoes flashing like a laser show. His sister squealed, sprinting to catch up, and both parents exchanged a harried look before chasing after them, shouting in vain for them to stop.

Did they have any clue how lucky they were? Their happiness appeared so seamless.

Would the camera be able to capture the perfection of that mayhem? Jacob didn't need to look at his wife to know she'd be feeling the same sense of loss as him right now. The same hurt that had torn them apart instead of bringing them together.

The task of welcoming so many happy couples was quickly creating a widening, consuming coil of decades of pain. He'd done his best to keep his wife safe and build the future they'd dreamed of.

And he'd failed.

What could he do to make up for that? What could he do to give her the happiness she deserved, even if that happiness didn't include him? He'd foolishly thought he'd found the magic formula for years only to be so very wrong, and now he only had two weeks left to persuade her to at least try the long-distance marriage angle.

A horn honked in the distance, then a second. Jacob looked over sharply. Three vans bearing the logo of the local child services and group home. Even from a distance, he could see little bodies bouncing in the seats with pent-up energy, some pressing their faces against the glass.

Hollie shot a quick look at Jacob. "If I'm going to stand a chance at making my costume change in time, you're going to have to help me get out of this dress."

Chapter Three

Jacob wished he had more than five minutes to enjoy helping his wife unfasten all those tiny pearly buttons stretching down her spine.

And while there were instances where he didn't mind passing off some duty to a trusted employee to give himself family time, today was different. Today was about the press and recognition for that for these kids. He couldn't save his family, his marriage. And he couldn't give to a child as a father the way he'd always dreamed. But he could help others find families by showcasing these children's needs to the community.

Sighing, Hollie fluffed her long brown hair,

and gentle waves tumbled over her subtly sinking shoulders. The gesture was small, barely noticeable. But Jacob knew the deeper meanings of all of Hollie's gestures. And this slight sag of her posture was an indicator of active heartache.

How he ached to pull her close and run his fingers up and down her back.

His wife's forehead furrowed. "Thank you for the help. I've got a few of our matching outfits that you never moved over to your suite. They're already pressed and ready to pick from—since we're short on time."

After a particularly ugly argument on the fifth anniversary of her cancer recovery, she'd evicted him from their suite and over to one of the guest quarters. He still couldn't untangle how, during a time they should have been celebrating her recovery, they'd ended up hurling ugly words and ultimatums. She'd even launched his suitcase and some of his clothes.

"Which ones?" he asked, since the look of her stepping out of the wedding dress dried up all other thoughts.

She draped the gown over the arm of the velvet sofa and strode over to the closet, then absently fingered the array of outfits.

"We have the red check shirts and the blue

with the embroidery." Calling over her shoulder, eyes catching his, she delivered her report flatly. Another signature move of Hollie's pain. "Or we could wear the denim with leather vests."

Jacob thought back to other moments they'd worn those outfits, remembering the first time they'd donned the complementary blue embroidered outfits. They were newlyweds then, back at a time when Hollie's laugh had been free and unguarded, lighting up a summer barn dance. He could hear the lilt of the guitar, still smell the sweetness of cherry pie on Hollie's lips.

An ache settled in his chest at the loss. But maybe, just maybe, old clothes could bestow new magic. Help him find a middle ground with Hollie that was less painful than this complete schism. "How about the blue? I think the kids will like all the stitching, and yours has the white fringe, too."

She froze in her tracks.

Then it hit him like a bull as to why. An image hammered him of her holding JJ, his little fingers twisting in the fringe. Hollie's laughter had filled the room and his heart as she tenderly eased the threads from his fierce tiny grip. Oh yes. He had forgotten that memory—no, scratch that. He actively pushed down those memories. The pain of losing JJ and then losing Hollie cut through him all over again.

She cleared her throat, face taut. "The blue it is, then. I'll be right back."

Regret pinched. He hated that, even unwittingly, he'd reminded her of the lost child that had still haunted their every interaction for the past year. Even now, it took a herculean effort to tamp down thoughts of their brief time as parents.

But he did it. Stopping the reminiscing was the only way to put one foot in front of the other.

Jacob gathered up her wedding dress and placed it carefully on the bed, the fabric still warm from her body. Indulging himself, he brought the lacy gown to his face, inhaling the lingering scent of her lilac body wash. Memories flooded him of showering together, of smoothing the bath gel over every inch of her body.

The sound of footsteps pulled him back to the present. He dropped the dress and pivoted just as she returned.

"All set?" he asked.

"Just about." She'd already changed into her navy-blue shirt with white embroidery and fringe. Delicately stitched flowers blossomed on the shirt. Denim hugged her long legs and hips. She clutched his outfit as she crossed to him, her black leather boots thudding along the thick rug.

Lordy, she was stunning regardless of whether she wore jeans or a lace gown. What would it take to persuade her to cancel their appointment to see the divorce attorney? Even revisiting the subject made his gut knot.

Needing something to lighten the pall settling over the room, he spread his arms wide. "If you want my help again…"

She shook her head fast, emphatically so. "I'm good. Thanks, though. I need to check in with Ashlynn." She shoved the hangers with his shirt and jeans against his chest. "And while I'm doing that, get dressed, cowboy. I'll meet you outside."

Her blue eyes flickered with something— awareness?—just before she pivoted away. Snagging her black Stetson from a hook on the wall, she made fast tracks away, the sweet curves of her bottom too enticing with the white stitching on her back pockets.

He shook off the distraction and hauled on his clothes with record speed, sparing only an instant to toss his wedding gear on top of her gown. What a sad parody of how their garments had ended up together twenty years ago.

This couldn't be all that was left of them. They'd

worked so hard and accomplished so much. They deserved to savor some kind of happiness together, however that came, for however long. He just had to set his mind to just the right angle that wouldn't spook his wary wife.

Slamming his black Stetson on his head, he charged through the French doors from his suite onto their private patio, hoping to catch up to her. Flanking oaks and crepe myrtles nestled together to form a small grove, casting shade over the stone paver circle. The trees were old, solid, with deep roots.

A few months ago, in another attempt to create peace, Jacob had reimagined this space with the help of their new landscaper, Charlotte, complete with a small butterfly house nestled into the greenery. He wanted a haven for Hollie filled with markers of life. Charlotte executed his vision, creating a "sniff-garden" safe for their many roaming animals. The area surrounding the base of the trees was overflowing with airy dill, aromatic rosemary, leafy clusters of purple basil, a small sea of catnip, blankets of deep green ferns.

Charlotte understood how important animals were to him and to Hollie and had taken great care to create a bin for dog toys as well as an elaborate, multilevel cat climbing tour. Two overstuffed lounge chairs huddled near the stone fire pit. Jacob had envisioned sharing glasses of wine with his wife and rekindling their marriage in this oasis.

What an epic fail.

Knowing time was short, he accelerated to a jog, carefully trekking along the flagstone path, boots drumming a steady pace. Stone statues of rabbits, deer, and foxes poked out from the billowing ferns.

Every step on the path reminded him of how many challenges lay before him. First and foremost, saying goodbye to his wife, waking up every day without her under their roof. His pace quickened. Jacob felt suddenly claustrophobic in the lush path. He needed more space, more air.

Did Hollie feel the same? Might they benefit from some time away from the ranch, even just a short picnic in one of their favorite spots? Something like that might go a long way toward showing her they could be partners without all the high drama and emotion.

He continued jogging down the flagstone path until he came upon Lonnie, one of the massage therapists. Lonnie had been a vital part of the Top Dog Ranch team from the start. The older man had often served as a friend and mentor to Jacob. And if there was ever a time Jacob could use a friend, it was now.

Jacob called, "Lonnie, hold up a minute and I'll walk with you."

"A minute is all I have, Boss. Patsy will kick my butt if I don't get this floral plan to the new landscaper right away." Lifting his cream-colored Stetson to wipe his brow, Lonnie let out a low whistle. "It's the details on greenery for our ceremony. We can't thank you enough for letting us renew our vows during the big spring weddings festival. We could have never afforded anything this nice on our own."

Jacob shot him a wry grin. "Is that a hint for a raise?"

They walked shoulder to shoulder on the path that snaked from the back of the grand lodge to the front.

"Wellllll," Lonnie said, arching a bushy gray eyebrow, "if you're offering…"

Chuckling, Jacob clapped him on the back as the front of the lodge came into view. Jacob noted the line of vans moving toward the drop-off area. "I can guarantee you that when money for raises is available, you and Patsy are tops on the list."

Lonnie's face smoothed, his bright blue eyes serious. "While that's nice to hear, I actually had something else in mind to talk to you about. Once the wedding is past, Patsy and I would like to discuss relocating to the new location."

Birdsong lingered on the chilly air, mingling with the sounds of the van engines. Trees cast long shadows on their walk.

"Really? I'm surprised you're considering moving. I thought you enjoyed being close to the grandchildren. Are they moving?"

Lonnie shook his head, sun gleaming off his trim white beard. "We love our job. The new outpost of the dude ranch just happens to be halfway between all our children. But if that's not an option, we will stay here rather than leave the Top Dog family."

"That's good to know. I appreciate your openness and your loyalty." He sifted the information in his head. There was no reason not to move them to the new location. He would simply hire a new massage therapy team for here. But Lord, he would miss them. "You and Patsy are like family. Of course, I want you to live wherever makes you happiest. I'm sure we can hammer out something for you there."

Lonnie and Patsy had been with them from the start, right there in the early days brainstorming pack-tivities and promotions. Every step of the way, they'd celebrated landmarks together. He thought of the couples' shower Patsy and Lonnie had hosted when JJ came into their lives.

They'd been the first to console them when JJ's birth mother took him back, grieving right alongside them over the loss of a baby they'd labeled as an honorary grandchild. Lonnie's support had been invaluable.

Jacob pulled at the sleeve of his fringe shirt. He wanted the best for his longtime employees who had become like family. But he couldn't ignore the twinge of loss.

It seemed everyone in his world—including his wife—was moving on. He refused to be left behind.

"Lonnie, I need a favor. Could you and Patsy cover for us tomorrow morning?"

Hollie had a pounding headache.

The stressful interaction with Jacob had her massaging her temples and craving ibuprofen. She wished she could offload some of the responsibilities to him, but this event meant too much to her to drop the ball. A showstopping welcome was crucial for setting the right tone.

At least the children were all unloaded from the vans. The three social workers—two older women and a younger gentleman—were corralling the excited kids as they raced around the courtyard, paw print name tags flapping.

Ashlynn had adjusted the welcome station into a more kid-friendly theme. The band still played on the wagon, children's songs. Tables on either side sported brown bag meals, each labeled with a child's name. A ranch employee dressed as a rodeo clown walked through the crowd, making balloon animals.

And the biggest attraction of all? Dog pens were set up with puppies from a local shelter prancing inside, volunteers from the shelter watching over them.

Jacob rushed up to her side, breathless and too handsome. He reached up and snagged the microphone from the lead singer and called for everyone's attention. "Welcome to the Top Dog Dude Ranch. I'm Jacob O'Brien, and this pretty lady…" He gestured to her. "This is my wife and favorite cowgirl, Hollie."

Pointing toward the pens with little fluffy canines, Hollie continued, "Who wants to see the puppies?"

Her question was answered by a cacophony of squeals and flash of bright eyes. A tanned girl with thick braids clapped her hands together. A few of the younger boys whooped, shaking their balloon dogs into the air. The shelter volunteers guided children over, giving them treats to share, letting them pet the pups as the adults held them.

Hollie leaned toward the photographer, who was snapping pictures at a breakneck speed. "We have our staff plus some volunteers from a local animal shelter, so there will be plenty of eyes on the children."

Jacob nodded. "And tonight after we eat, there's a petting zoo."

Shawna, the head counselor and their primary point of contact, swiped a hand over her harried brow, pushing back her lovely coils of hair. "That all sounds perfect. It'll be just what they need to help get their wriggles out while we check in."

Hollie gestured toward a table full of brown sacks with names written on paw print stickers. "Our assistant over there—Ashlynn—has your dinner bags. Each one is labeled. All the children's dietary restrictions have been taken into account and noted." She lost herself in details and routine to keep from soaking up the sight of her husband kneeling to scoop up a lost balloon animal for a gap-toothed boy. "Picnic grounds have been roped off just for the kids in your group, no other guests in that section. Just to confirm again, no one with peanut allergies, correct?"

Shawna offered with a nod and a smile. "That's right. And it's a rarity, for sure."

Hollie continued, "You'll see in your welcome packet the assigned pack-tivities set to start tomorrow. First up, they'll put their new cowboy hats to good use with pony rides. They'll be able to rope a fake steer and take scooter rides around barrels."

Watching all the children as the counselor checked off names on the list, Hollie felt such a mishmash of emotions, joy and pain. She might be in a hurry to wrap up her time at the ranch so she could start her next chapter, but this meant something to her. She wouldn't shortchange the kids, no matter how difficult it was to be around Jacob.

The counselor never took her gaze off clusters of children in the open area. A balloon animal held by one of the younger girls popped. The rodeo clown rushed over, hands quickly twisting a replacement. The girl in pigtails smiled brightly at the new animal—a pink cat.

"You're certainly starting them off with the full Western experience." She hugged her clipboard to her chest. "You've thought of everything."

Jacob winked. "This isn't our first rodeo."

Shawna's chestnut-colored eyes gleamed. "Well, it sure looks to me like you understand children."

He winced. Hollie felt his flinch all the way to her toes. But she pulled a tight smile. It served nothing for her to share her heartache with this woman she'd just met. Talking about it hurt too much. People offered consolation, shallow words like how at least she'd survived the cancer that left her barren. As year after year in remission went by, she'd been thankful, finally ready to adopt.

Life had sure given her a bait and switch.

Hollie hauled her attention back to the present and all the heartbreakingly precious children.

Shawna pressed her palm to her chest. Gratitude radiated from her smile. She looked back the children laughing and playing. "Thank you for making this vacation possible."

"It's our joy." Hollie's mouth felt impossibly dry, and her heart started beating overtime.

"This is more than just a camp voucher or trip to an amusement park. The healing-based pack-tivities you offer make this the perfect place for the children to get some additional help, help that many of them won't accept in a traditional thera-peutic setting. Thank you."

All Hollie could manage was a small smile and a nod of acknowledgment. The constriction in her chest increased. She breathed in for a count of four and exhaled for a count of five. She wanted to run hard and fast to find the next yoga class by the pond, but she had work to do.

Shawna continued, tilting her head to the group of children closet to them. "Over there, that little toddler—" she pointed to a tow-headed boy with a shaky walk "—is Ezra. He was born with neurological issues stemming from drug use during pregnancy. And those four are the Hudson siblings. Elliot Hudson will only speak to animals."

Hollie watched the way Elliot, who couldn't be older than four years old, plop down, snuggling into his parrot balloon animal. "I guess he's come to the right place."

Lips tight, Shawna tucked her tablet in her bag. "I hear it said that all these kids need is love and a family. But truly, they need—they deserve—so much more to help them process all they've been through."

Hollie's throat clogged with emotion. She hoped the press from this trip would bring new homes for the kids, and yes, she wished she and Jacob could have offered to be that family for a child. But she couldn't survive having her heart shredded again. She would do what she could for these kids in other ways, like this event that was happening at the worst possible time.

Her attention lingered on Elliot and his siblings. The way they formed a small unit. The girl wearing thick glasses appeared to be around five or six, a little older than her brother. She handed over her blue dog balloon animal to Elliot. A smile lit his green eyes as he arranged his parrot and dog in a row.

"Hollie?"

Blinking fast, she looked up to find Ashlynn beside her. The alarm on her assistant's face sent a bolt of panic crackling along Hollie's already ragged nerves.

What now?

Ashlynn leaned in to whisper, "I just got word that the main freezer's broken."

The one jam-packed full of food prepared for the upcoming events.

Hollie's headache pounded harder as she turned to the counselor. "It's been wonderful meeting you, Shawna. If you need anything at all, my assistant, Ashlynn, can help you. Her personal cell number is in your welcome packet."

Grinding her teeth in frustration, Hollie pressed her fingers to her temples. Sure, this was a minor inconvenience in the big scheme of things, but she was so depleted, even a minor snafu felt like her legs had been kicked out from under her. They'd been through so much tragedy and trauma in their marriage. She just wanted some peace.

Jacob rubbed along her back, his strong hand knowing just where to go to ease the tension, even as another, heated tension sneaked in to take its place. "It'll be okay."

"It's like the appliances have created a suicide pact and they're all going to kick the bucket at once. Gallons of churned ice cream will melt if we don't act fast." All the ice cream had been made from scratch, no easy feat given how much they'd planned to serve with a full guest list. She'd worked long hours at the ice cream shop, storing the extra at the main lodge so they would have enough for this event. She sighed, taking the microphone from him and turning to the kids. "Who wants ice cream?"

"Me, me, me…" The chant rippled through the crowd, hands rising.

Jacob tucked his head close to hers, the brim of his Stetson hiding his scowl from the others and reached to turn off the mic. "How are we supposed to make that happen? It'll take forever to load them up—if we can even pry them away from the puppies."

Hollie answered, "You and Lonnie could bring it here. I'll call the chef to make an adjustment in the dinner menu, too, so all the pie for the wedding parties is à la mode. At least then it won't go to waste. We can sort out later how to shift the snacks and desserts we were originally going to serve."

His scowl faded, and he studied her through narrowed eyes, assessing. "We make a good team, you know. Seems a shame to break up that partnership."

Seriously? What was he thinking? And why did he have to bring it up now?

It was probably just his libido talking.

"We'll adapt," she rebuffed him dryly.

A spark lit in his deep brown eyes, and just as he knew where to rub her back, she understood his moods. He wasn't angry. He was turned on by her sassy answer. The embers of the fire between them had been fanned in countless ways today, not the least of which, standing in front of him in nothing but her underwear.

A tingle climbed up her spine, along her arms. Heaven help her, she wanted to sway into him for a kiss that had nothing to do with photoshoots and everything to do with indulging in one last lip-lock with her husband.

A tug on her sleeve captured her attention, the

white fringe swaying with the unexpected movement. She cleared her mind of wayward thoughts about Jacob that would only lead to more heartache.

Work.

That was her life now.

The tug grew more insistent. She looked down to see an adorable little girl with a polka-dot bow in her hair, clutching a toy lasso to her chest.

"Are you going to be my new mommy and daddy?"

Chapter Four

Freddy Hudson hated suck-ups.

And that little girl with polka-dot ribbon in her hair was one of the biggest suck-ups he'd ever met. Isabella grinned at the ranch owners, hugging her pink lasso like it was all she'd ever dreamed of owning, even though Freddy knew she liked finger painting best.

Licking his strawberry ice-cream cone, he dropped to sit on a bale of hay, far away from everyone else. He didn't want to play all these stupid cowboy games. That wasn't even a real cow over there. Just a barrel with horns and a saddle.

But Isabella was pretending. She probably

wanted extra sprinkles on her double scoop of boring old vanilla.

After six months in a group home, he'd seen kids doing whatever they could to win over somebody so they could go home with new parents. He didn't want new parents.

He just wanted his old ones back.

But since that couldn't happen, he figured he was better off making sure he was such a pain in the butt that nobody asked for him. Being bad was the only thing that made him feel better these days, made him feel a little less mad at the world.

Although he would still be mad at Isabella.

Freddy adjusted his backwards baseball cap, the one his real dad had given him before everything changed and he, his little sister and his younger twin brothers got stuck in that crummy place.

From his spot on the hay bale, he could check out the whole crowd. And all these other kids made him roll his eyes. Hard. They were being saps and attention hogs.

Why didn't people notice his little sister? Sure, Ivy's bows came untied as soon as she moved, and she had chocolate ice cream all over her face, but she was sweet, and she didn't beg for attention all the time like Isabella. At least Ivy was happy, quietly holding a little brown puppy.

Her head was down, and she looked like she mighta been singing to the dog. She did that a lot—sang songs like their mom used to do at bedtime.

He scanned the crowd to find his twin brothers. Elliot and Phillip jumped around, dancing in front of the band. They weren't identical—in looks or in the way they acted.

As the oldest, he needed to watch out for them. It didn't matter that he was only seven and they were four. Ivy was five. And even though she was smart enough to be twice that age, he was the man in the family now.

Hay rustled next to Freddy. Who had found him way back here? To his surprise, it was the ranch owner, a muscley man with dark brown hair. He tipped his Stetson.

Mr. O'Brien settled onto the bale of hay beside him. "Are you lost, cowboy?"

Cowboy? Was this guy for real? Freddy kept on staring at the crowd. "Nope. Just eating my ice cream. In peace. Where I don't have to share."

His ice cream was almost gone. Two more licks and he would be crunching on the wafer sugar cone. His stomach growled lightly. He wished he had a second scoop, but he wasn't asking anybody for anything. It was better than being told no. And he was tired of asking for every little thing in his life like people were doing him a favor giving him a stupid toothbrush.

"I can get more for you if you want. The ice-cream shop is run by my wife."

"I think your wife is busy giving away all the ice cream to that little girl." Freddy scrunched his nose in disgust. "Isabella."

"She's a cute kid."

"Isabella hit my little sister." He bit into the cone, melted ice cream oozing out of the bottom onto his hand.

"That's not nice at all." Mr. O'Brien passed him a handkerchief covered in a puppy print pattern.

Freddy took it warily, wiping off his fingers. He let out a sigh. He was still really angry at Isabella. And at himself for getting in trouble. "She didn't get caught like I did."

"You didn't hit her back, did you?" he asked softly, not angry-like, but still a caution.

"No, my dad says boys never hit girls." The admission jabbed at his heart. He stuffed the rest of the soggy cone in his mouth.

"Your father was right." Mr. O'Brien nodded. He didn't seem like the judgy kind of adult.

But still, Freddy just wanted to be left alone. He wasn't going to talk about his dad. Especially not with this guy.

Freddy swallowed in a gulp. "So, I put a frog down Isabella's shirt."

Mr. O'Brien laughed for a second before he covered his mouth and smoothed away his smile. "Did you get in trouble?"

"Yep. She didn't, though. And now she's eating all the ice cream. That's really not fair. Except my dad always said life isn't fair."

That was for sure.

Mr. O'Brien stretched his legs out in front of him, crossing his booted feet all casual-like. "What happened to your father, if you don't mind my asking?"

Freddy minded. A lot. "My dad and my mom work on a cruise ship. They'll be back to get us by Christmas."

He threw down the bandanna on the bale of hay and shot to his feet. If this guy thought that a few days in some fairy-tale, make-believe camp would fix things, he didn't deserve a real answer. And Freddy didn't want his ice cream or his pretend happily-ever-after.

Last week, Jacob would have welcomed the excuse of a broken freezer as an opportunity not to spend awkward time alone with Hollie. But since walking in on her wearing her wedding grown—

then wearing far less—he wanted to see if the awareness in her eyes was for real.

And more importantly, see if it could be rekindled for them to find their way to some kind of marriage of convenience.

Instead, he was stuck dismantling a freezer at ten o'clock at night. Two years ago, he would have just bought another one without a second thought. But the expansion had left them a bit strapped for cash, and he'd already purchased a new industrial fridge and freezer for the other facility.

Lucky for him, one of their new guests—Thomas—had overheard about the problem and offered his assistance, along with proof of his contractor's license. Jacob had been stunned by the generous offer, but the older man had insisted, and the regular repairman wasn't available until first thing the next morning. Thomas's help was a godsend.

Perhaps a little bit of that Top Dog magic was sparkling their way for a change?

Jacob wiped the sweat from his brow as Thomas arranged tools on a tarp laid out on the ground of the lodge's kitchen that was normally accessible twenty-four hours a day for all guests.

"Thomas, remind me to give you a voucher for

a trip to the gift shop. You shouldn't have to work on your vacation."

As he surveyed the kitchen, Jacob felt his usual determination falter. So much food crowded the black-and-white granite countertops. Thomas's fiancée was helping Ashlynn and Hollie, all three women quick on their feet. Their objective was to cook or bake as much of the thawing food as they could to keep it from spoiling. They'd already packed every available freezer space in the smaller appliances, and still all of this was leftover due to booking two such massive events at the same time.

While Jacob stood next to Thomas, who adjusted the straps on his overalls, Hollie and the other women set up shop at the kitchen table. Baking dishes for coffee cake, muffins, and doggy treats were strewn everywhere.

Chaos. There was no other way to describe the scene. Much like in the beginning of the operation, when he and Hollie had done the remodel of this space themselves.

Everywhere he turned, he found ghosts of his past stirring. Memories of Hollie singing along to the blaring radio while they laid tile flashed in his mind. He stole a glance across the room to where Hollie worked with Connie and Ashlynn to salvage the rapidly thawing ingredients. She still wore her blue shirt, the white fringe a blur as she stirred blueberry muffins.

Thomas squatted behind the freezer, sleeves rolled up. "I like to stay busy. No offense meant, but coming here is Connie's dream."

"No offense taken." Jacob passed a wrench. "We hear that a lot from wedding couples. Although by the end of the trip, they've found we have plenty to offer for R & R."

The air was scented with cinnamon and sugar, by-products of the frantic baking. Scents that would always remind him of his wife.

As if pulled by a magnetic force, Jacob turned toward Hollie. Her blue eyes met his. A sense of a spark rippled through him as her gaze dipped to his bare arms. Jacob's biceps twitched in response in the white T-shirt. He'd discarded his blue shirt on the back of one of the tree trunk barstools. Jacob felt the air freeze in his lungs as if an exhale would break this small spell.

Breath, it turned out, wouldn't be the breaker of this moment. Duty was. Thomas held out a hand and tapped Jacob's leg—signaling that he needed to be handed a tool.

Jacob passed a screwdriver to the older gentleman, eyes falling away from Hollie and skimming over the doggy gate and down the hall that led back to their private quarters. How he wanted to disappear with Hollie down that corridor, past Bandit, who was curled up snoozing by the short gate.

Thomas worked quickly and deftly, his comfort with the job apparent. "To be fair, I was relieved at the location. I was worried her princess wedding would involve going to some hoity-toity place with lots of lace and crystal and tea parties."

"No worries there, my friend."

Angling his wrench, Thomas loosened a covering on the back of the freezer. His mouth was open as he huffed, straining with the too-tight bolt. The access panel begrudgingly gave way, and Thomas nodded mostly to himself at the success. "The Top Dog Dude Ranch is a great compromise with the horses and ranching theme. I can't wait to get out on the trails."

He understood better than most how healing time on horseback could be. How many times had Jacob found solace on the trails this last year?

"There is no lack of terrain or vistas on our trails." Jacob wished he could have convinced Hollie to ride with him more often, but their way of dealing with their grief had been so different, it felt like nothing he suggested helped. "Have you ridden much?"

Thomas made quick work of the screws holding down the framework around the compressor. "I grew up on a cattle farm where my dad was the foreman. He started me out in the saddle early. It was tough when he got multiple sclerosis and had to retire early."

"That's rough. I'm sorry."

"That's life. You move on. That's what my dad always said." His shoulders shrugged as stood, making his way toward the tarp and toolbox. He pulled a few pliers and screwdrivers out before returning.

Hollie had said a variation on that same notion when he'd tried to tell her that they try adoption again. She'd told him he should move on with his life—without her.

The slice of her words had cut deeply. They still did.

Jacob cleared his throat. "Well, here's a tip. When you're ready to hit the trails, be sure to ask to saddle up Goliath." He made a point to know the riding aptitude of each of their guests while still having the stable staff monitor the fit. Goliath was a large Tennessee walking horse, but he was also calm and steady. "He's one of our newer horses and an absolute favorite of mine."

They'd acquired so many animals of late,

getting ready for the expansion. A part of him mourned the loss of those early days when the business had been smaller. He didn't want to lose that family feel. But that felt like an impossible goal when his actual family was fracturing.

All the more reason to hold on to whatever connections he could with his wife. He just had to be patient until he found just the right way to help her see that while their old dreams were gone, they could still salvage something.

While still protecting their embattled hearts.

Hollie was used to working long hours, but her energy tank was just about empty. And she wasn't anywhere near done baking coffee cakes and muffins.

The morning of wedding photos, followed by a day of welcoming children in need of families and happy couples, disturbed her fragile hold on acceptance of the soon-to-be divorced life sprawling before her.

And the freezer still wasn't running, in spite of Jacob and Thomas's best efforts.

Half listening to Ashlynn make conversation with Connie, Hollie poured the batter into miniloaf pans. She had prepared the batter in advance and frozen it to save time during large events, a plan that worked well until days like today. They couldn't afford to throw all of it out, which meant she was going to be baking well into the night. She just had to hunker down and plow through.

At least she wasn't alone with Jacob here in the kitchen. She appreciated his willingness to work hard to problem-solve when the business was in crisis, a quality she'd always admired. So it had surprised her when their personal crisis had left them reacting so differently. She thought she had come to peace with her decision to let him go so he could move on with his life.

Too much had happened today, leaving her nerves raw and ragged. Peace was more elusive than ever.

Hollie pushed the beagle-shaped cookie jar to the side, giving herself more room as she worked to salvage something from this nightmare. Rolling her wrists with practiced ease, she whisked together the next batch of coffee cakes. Ashlynn gathered two pans of baked goodies—pup-cake pops for dogs and the first of the coffee cakes for humans—and headed toward the stainless steel industrial ovens. Ashlynn's eyes were full of determination when she turned back from setting the pans on the racks.

Her assistant fished her phone from her jeans

pocket, scanning a recently created checklist for this unfolding crisis. Hollie looked at the ingredients piled on the counter and flicked her gaze back to Ashlynn. An owl hooted from somewhere outside the lodge. Yet another reminder of how late the night grew. Hollie felt bad for asking her to work such long hours when Ashlynn used her evenings to finish up her college degree in business.

But they had to dig in.

Connie leaned on her elbows, watching with genuine interest as Hollie carefully and precisely poured batter into the next vacant coffee cake tray. Even in the subdued light, a flush colored Connie's fair cheeks as she glanced over at her fiancé helping Jacob. Joy etched into her smile lines as she spoke. "Any advice for a soon-to-be newlywed? You two sure do look to have an amazing partnership."

Run?

Probably not what the woman wanted to hear, so Hollie settled for a more benign answer, one she'd used countless times in the past when Top Dog guests commented on their marriage. "Marriages are complicated. Business is easy."

They'd proven they could build a business from the ground up. Many rooms and nooks in the Top Dog Dude Ranch were testaments to their matched business savvy partnership. But the kitchen show-cased the care that existed between them best. Arranged in gallery walls, paw prints, dog portraits, and dog themed plaques—a representation of decades of joint collecting.

Hand-painted signs read, *Home is where the dog is*, or *Love is a four-legged word*, or *Live, Love, Bark*. Jacob had brought this last sign back as a present their third year of marriage when he traveled to purchase six horses.

Heartbeat fluttering, she touched her rib cage, and her eyes drifted to Jacob as he worked with Thomas. She'd always preferred him like this—wearing a plain white T-shirt, working with his hands. For Hollie, Jacob's steady demeanor had made him home to her. Maybe that's why it had been so hard to feel lost and alone in her grief. Jacob hadn't been there for her the way she needed, and the loss of her home—her sense that he was there for her no matter what—had shattered irreparably.

The sense of loss rose in her throat, bile burning. She swallowed hard, to no avail.

"Well," Connie said, "you two have sure made a shining example. I hear you're even expanding. That's just remarkable, especially at a time when so many businesses are closing down."

Scraping the side of the glass bowl with a spatula, Hollie guided the last bits of the batter into paw-print-shaped muffin tins, multitasking back and forth with making coffee cakes and muffins. "We've had a detailed plan for the ranch right from the start, complete with stages of expansion." Her cancer battle had set them back in time and money. And once they caught back up, JJ was taken back by his birth mother, and there was no marriage left to save. She wiped her hands on a cream-colored hand towel. "I used to worry that if we took on more, we wouldn't have any time for each other."

"How long have you been married?" Her gaze gravitated to Thomas.

"We've been married for two decades, together much longer than that." She swallowed down the ache of nostalgia.

"How did you meet?" Connie pressed.

Rather than risk being rude, Hollie let herself be drawn into the memory. "I was only sixteen when he walked into my daddy's ice-cream parlor. He placed his order and asked me out all in one breath."

He'd ordered a double scoop of chocolate ice cream in a waffle cone. He'd always had a sweet tooth, right down to licking the bowl when she baked.

"Wow, grass doesn't grow under his feet." Connie fanned her face with a pot holder. "And then you lived happily ever after. How romantic."

"Well, I said no." Hollie couldn't hold back a smile. "And continued to say no when he came to the shop once each week to ask me out again."

Memories rolled through her mind, frame after frame, of those happy months spent learning about Jacob. She'd tried to be practical about their relationship even then, unwilling to be impulsive no matter how much he appealed to her. But he'd patiently won her over, his persistence one of his most endearing qualities.

Or at least it had been.

"How long did it take you to say yes? I assume you said yes eventually since you're married," Connie teased.

"Four months and three weeks." Hollie reached for the pottery bowl full of the cinnamon and brown sugar topping. "Each week he would share something about himself and ask me about my life. But it wasn't the things he told me that won me over. It was seeing the way he treated other people when he thought I wasn't looking."

"What a lovely insight."

A lump stuck in her throat, and she focused overlong on the baking to hide her face.

Jacob still was kind that way, which is what made their breakup all the more difficult. There was no one to cast as the villain, except for fate. Blinking once, then twice, Hollie looked up from the muffin tins to meet Connie's green eyes. "But that's enough about my life. Tell me how you and Thomas met. I want to hear about your romance."

"Well, it was quite simple, really. I'm a nurse in a family practice. The refrigerator with all of our medications went on the fritz, and Thomas rode in to save the day. He had everything up and running in no time." She smiled, her eyes taking on a faraway look. "On his way out, he asked for my personal cell phone number. To celebrate the one year anniversary of the day that we met, he proposed."

"That's very romantic—a true love at first sight."

"We may not have known each other for as long as you and Jacob, but the moment I saw him, it felt like I'd known him for my entire life."

Connie touched a hand to her chest and looked to where Thomas worked. Her admiration and love were apparent in her delicate face and softly upturned lips. Hadn't Hollie looked at Jacob that way before, too?

Hollie's gaze tracked to her husband, her mind full of memories of those teenage years when he'd romanced her. Little had she known that his persistence then would prove to be such a problem later. He just couldn't accept the answer no.

She might have stayed in that daydream, that sweet-scented memory, too. But she couldn't linger in memories of the past with so much baking to do tonight.

Tough to do with the distraction of Jacob's biceps pressed against the sleeves of his shirt.

No one could live in those moments long-term, though. Especially not when the forces of the universe seemed to have decided now was the best time for trials of all sorts. Top Dog magic seemed well out of reach for her and Jacob.

Ashlynn darted across the room, her cell phone grasped tightly in her hand. And she had that wary look again. Ugh.

"Hollie, I hate to interrupt…"

What now? "Yes? Is everything okay with the food?"

Hollie looked fast from the coffee cakes she was preparing at the counter to the other loaves and muffins cooling on the racks, perfect color on top. Others were still in the oven.

Ashlynn waggled her cell phone. "Forget about the baking. I've got one of the counselors on the line. She says that little boy who was acting up earlier—Freddy—has climbed out the bunkhouse window."

Chapter Five

Hollie's heart still hammered against her rib cage even though they'd located the little runner. After racing over, they'd learned Freddy had managed to jimmy the window of the guest quarters and shimmy out, but hadn't made it further than the bunkhouse railing, thanks to the alarm system. But her brain still churned with what-if scenarios.

Now, Hollie paced off nervous energy on the porch, waiting while the counselor—Shawna—finished tucking in all the children and doing an additional head count in both bunkhouses. They'd erected the two additional structures nearly ten years ago to accommodate retreats, summer camps, and family reunions. Jacob climbed a step-ladder to check the security along the top of each window. He had to be totally fried. She was certainly brain-dead from exhaustion.

Shawna's bright eyes still glinted with fear, and cool white floodlights illuminated creases on her brow. Wind stirred the pink streak in her light brown hair. She approached them on heavy foot-falls, pulling on a sweater. "I am so sorry for sending up the alert prematurely."

Hollie waved a hand before pressing into the center of her chest. Fringe coils tickled the insides of her wrists. "I'm just glad the little boy is okay."

Shawna plowed a shaky hand through her hair. "We have a dozen protocols in place to keep watch over these kids. I've been doing this job for twenty-five years, and I've never come across an escape artist like Freddy Hudson."

"What can we do to help you?" Hollie asked.

"The alarms on the windows were invaluable." Shawna crossed her arms over her chest with a weary sigh. "Thank you."

"We put those in a few years ago as an extra level of security for our younger patrons."

Shutter hinges creaked as Hollie watched Jacob check each window, muscles flexing. A small smile spread across her lips—against her will but unstoppable. Her eyes lingered on his methodical movements as he continued down the lodge. He'd always been so handsome, larger than life and oh so very capable. And right now, she was grateful for that strength, that steadiness in a crisis.

Child safety was tantamount. Hollie shuddered to imagine how differently it could have turned out. All of the children had wrist bands identifying them, including a contact phone number. She tried to think of what else could be done and came up blank. "Please let us know if you come up with any ideas for ways that we can assist you with the children."

"I appreciate your working with us and not just booting us out. Freddy is struggling with the transition into our group home, which is totally understandable, of course."

"Of course," Hollie echoed.

Starlight and a full moon drenched the ground. Shadows stretched from the wood line toward them. Maybe additional spotlights along the perimeter would help?

"We see children who grieve even the loss of a bad home—that's family and familiarity to them. But the parents of the four Hudson children were amazing." Sighing, she sagged back against the rail as a rustle sounded from the juniper bushes.

"Freddy, Ivy, Elliot, and Phillip had an idyllic life and that was abruptly and cruelly snatched away."

"Elliot is the little boy who only speaks to animals, right?" Hollie thought back to the twin with spiky hair who'd clutched the balloon animal to his chest like a lifeline.

"That's right." Shawna nodded, chewing a fingernail nervously.

"We have a school librarian who reads to the kids with our dogs present. Maybe Elliot would like one of the pups to be his buddy for story time." She also made a mental note to arrange special time for him with a new foal.

Shawna looked toward the bushes as the soft rustling continued. Over the past two decades, Hollie had learned the subtle differences between foxes, coyotes and raccoons moving through the woods. The small sounds she heard now were definitely the sounds of a mischievous raccoon moving through the dark.

"I think he would enjoy that," Shawna agreed, picking at her chewed-down nails. "The group home is particularly tough for a child like Freddy who acts out. We don't like to split up siblings, but there are four of them, and his brother has special needs. We're trying our best to work a solution for them." She shook her head, sighing hard. "Pardon me for unloading. It's been a long day. I just need to get some sleep, and I'm sure you do as well."

Hollie touched Shawna's arm lightly. "Please don't apologize. I admire your dedication to the job. Over two decades? You should be teaching classes around here about how to cope with stress."

"It's the children who are coping with the most. I get to go home at night to my husband and my dogs and my happy, normal life."

"It's good you're able to keep perspective. I would imagine the burnout rate is high in your profession."

Shawna fidgeted with the sleeves on her sweater. "You wouldn't know it, but sometimes the ones who aren't acting out are struggling just as hard, compensating. Isabella—the one who loves polka-dot hair bows—has been in four different homes since she was taken into custody. Her mother left her alone for hours at a time. Her defense? She would stockpile bottles in the crib so Isabella could feed herself. Isabella was nine months old."

Hollie swallowed down bile. She would have given her life for JJ—she still would. It was incomprehensible that anyone would behave so neglectfully to a tiny life entrusted to them.

Her gaze skirted to her broad-shouldered husband, who was currently climbing down the ladder. He'd moved heaven and earth to keep custody of JJ. How was he holding up seeing all of these heart-tugging little ones?

She'd thought powering through all these weddings was the worst thing possible to face. Little did she know, there was far worse in store to torment her heart.

If she was going to get through the next two weeks with her emotional well-being intact, she had to be careful about how much time she spent around the children. The reminders were so painful, and her heart still too raw. For now, she needed to stay as far away as possible from those pint-sized heart-tuggers.

As the sun climbed in the sky the next morning, Jacob felt determination settle into his bones. He needed to woo Hollie. Not in some romantic, hearts and flowers way, pushing for a grand love.

But in a way that stressed their shared bond of friendship—and chemistry.

With each passing moment showcasing all they'd built with the ranch, he became more certain it would be silly to just throw away their life. So what if it wasn't a fairy tale? If they both had the space of working at the different locations, they might be able to hold on to the remnants of their relationship.

The night before, she'd bolted from the bunkhouse before he could talk to her about having lunch together. Then she'd disappeared after breakfast, too. He would have thought she was avoiding him, except when he'd called her, he realized she'd left her phone on her desk, which was completely unlike her.

He needed to find her. So he'd resorted to the next best thing to a locator. He put a leash on their four-year-old border collie, Ziggy. The dog tipped his nose to the wind, sniffing left and right, then leading the way. Bandit howled from the kennel run attached to the barn, even though the voices of one of the stable hands echoed with soothing words and promises of treats.

Jacob mumbled under his breath while texting instructions for the staff to cover for him. "Next time, pup. I promise."

Ziggy's ears flicked back as he led them past the stables, where their horses softly nickered. The collie's tail stayed at attention as they continued forward past the admiring coos of guests. Ziggy was a handsome pup that often drew visitor's eyes and smiles.

Tucking his cell in his back pocket, he followed

Ziggy along the wooded path. With each step further, Jacob grew more and more certain of Hollie's location. Trees rustled while birdsong echoed. The mulchy scent of spring filled Jacob's nostrils with every inhale.

Ziggy pulled on the leash, his pace quickening on the dusty trail, leaving paw prints in his wake.

As they walked deeper into the woods, Jacob knew where he'd find Hollie. Ziggy led him to the mouth of the cave. Just like the doe of so long ago that had led his ancestor to this same spot to discover a puppy and Sulis Springs—to discover healing—Ziggy had brought him here.

And without question, Jacob knew Hollie was inside.

The space sprawled out, lit by dim lights recessed in stone, showcasing the springs bubbling. The walls were covered in eco-friendly paint, artwork created by the guests. Pottery was stacked in the corner, also made by Top Dog patrons.

So often he had come to the springs with Hollie when it was closed to visitors. Once upon a time, they'd made a point of sectioning off time for themselves, soaking in the warm and calming steam. They'd found their way back here at times they needed to heal, for two decades.

They'd also come here to make love.

Although odds were far greater that Hollie's visit here today had something to do with the former, because there wasn't a chance this was an invitation to get naked.

Low on the cave walls, lights flickered. Years ago, the fixtures were installed not only for safety but also for ambience. Today, the low lights cast Hollie in an ethereal glow. She seemed like a cave spirit or water nymph the way she sat at the edge of the spring, her dark-wash jeans rolled and cuffed, feet bare and submerged in the steaming waters. Her boots were positioned neatly beside her as her gaze fixed steadily on the spring.

"Hollie?" he called out, his voice echoing softly through the cavern. "Is something wrong?"

Her head was bowed, her dark waves obscuring all the delicate features of her face except for her sensuous lips. A Southwestern print serape in rich red hues wrapped around her shoulders, while the heels of her palms pressed in the rocky lip of the cave. Her feet dipped in and out of the water. Soft sounds of splashing water echoed gently in the cavern.

She looked up at him, despair tingeing her bright blue eyes even as her mouth formed a wobbly smile. "I'm sorry for worrying you. I'll be back in time to help with Allegra's bridal shower. I just needed a moment away from it all."

An ache settled in his gut, a deep sadness for his wife, but alongside that, a wariness on how to proceed. He'd never been able to help her through the pain before. They hadn't been able to grieve together— He stopped the thought short. To be fair, he hadn't been able to grieve alongside her. He'd ached to protect her and hadn't wanted to burden her further.

And in the end, that had pushed them so very far apart.

"I'm not worried about that. I asked Lonnie and Patsy to step in for the pony rides with the kids, and Ashlynn is handling the bridal brunch for the chia cake couple."

"Perfect. Thank you," she said quietly, her voice flat. Ziggy sidled up to her, pressing against her. She rested her head lightly on his. "Thanks for checking on me. You can go on back."

Jacob passed over her cell phone. "You forgot this. I wouldn't want you to get stranded out here."

"Oh, thanks." She took the device from him and set it beside her. "I must have been distracted."

"You're rarely distracted." It took something significant to throw his wife off her game. "So, I'll ask again, Hollie. What's wrong?"

She sat without speaking for so long, he wondered if she would ignore him outright. She'd done so in the past, but only at times her grief ran deeper than ever. So he sat on a flat rock near her, and he wasn't budging.

Still, the silence stretched and called attention to all the distance between them these past few years. The gentle sounds of the bubbling spring created a melancholy melody as he waited for his wife to speak.

Jacob heard Hollie swallow as he turned his head to take her in. Her chin quivered, and she turned her face to him, tears gathering in her eyes. "Jacob, I don't think I can do this."

Jacob ran a thumb over the top of her hand. "I know the weddings are tough, but—"

She pressed her palms to her cheeks for a shaky breath. "It's not that."

"Then what, babe?"

A choked sob slid between her lips. "I can't watch all of these children who've been through so much. I can't watch how the system has failed them and wonder if JJ is going to end up in foster care one day."

Horror rocked through him at even the thought. He thought about that little boy, Freddy. The child had vowed he was only going outside for a walk, but Jacob couldn't help but wonder what upset him enough to leave his siblings.

Every cell in him cried out in denial of JJ ever landing in foster care. "That's not possible."

"Isn't it? His biological mother already gave him up once. What if she does it again? Would they even notify us?" Her words picked up speed with the rising pitch of panic in her voice. "I don't know how to trust…anything."

He hauled her to his chest. She arched away for a moment. Then the resistance faded from her as she crumpled, sobbing into his chest.

Her tears tore him apart, reminding him of how he'd failed at keeping his family together. And as much as he'd wanted to give adoption another try, seeing how destroyed she still was over losing JJ? He couldn't ask her to go through that heartache again. He'd been wrong to push her.

Had he done so out of a misguided notion that a child would bind her to him? If so, he'd done her an even greater disservice—and if she'd said yes, he would have done a disservice to a child.

Guilt hammered him.

She blinked fast against the gathering tears, her face frozen in so much sorrow it was like a punch in his gut. She swiped away her teardrops with the tail of her wrap. "I'm sorry for falling apart like that. I've got it out now, and I'm better. I can handle it. I won't let down everyone at the ranch." She smoothed her wrap back in place. "Now, what did you want?"

Her? He wanted her.

But if he admitted as much, he would lose any chance at all with her. Or worse yet, she would think he was taking advantage of her tears, of her grief.

He needed to keep it simple, while still moving forward. If nothing else, he wanted to help her find her footing again, to make peace with their loss so she could heal. "I came to take you on a picnic."

"A picnic?" She choked on a watery laugh. "Are you crazy? We don't have time for that."

"Sure we do. Remember? Our awesome staff has it covered. That frees us to snag a quick brunch away from things before the Rossis renew their wedding vows." He lifted a hand. "Before you object, we were out late dealing with the freezer. Then securing the bunkhouse to keep the little escape artist secure. We've had more stress than anyone here knows. We need to regroup."

Chewing on her bottom lip, she burrowed her fingers in Ziggy's fur. "I wouldn't disagree about needing to regroup. But why on a picnic? Together?

Shouldn't we each take some time away—alone—
rather than stage more fake romance kisses?"

He told himself not to be disappointed in her
response. He could focus on something besides
romance. They weren't fighting. That was a win.

"Because then Milo wouldn't be able to photo-
graph us having a romantic picnic. It will be great
PR. And no kissing, nothing physical."

Unless she asked.

He could see he'd made progress. He understood her well. She couldn't deny a business opportunity.

Little did she know, he intended for the outing
to be far from business and all about the personal.

What in the world did Jacob have planned?

This outing was starting to seem a lot more than
just a simple picnic for promo. With each mile of his
truck eating up the miles, she grew more certain.

Hollie had been married to him long enough
to know when he had an ulterior motive. He was
never obvious. She had to look closely to catch
that glint in his eyes, note the way he covered his
mouth as if to hide a smile.

But she couldn't find a valid reason to say no to
his picnic idea, not when the photographer would
be documenting.

So she'd piled into Jacob's F-350, dogs loaded up in the back seat, a picnic basket strapped down in the truck bed. Milo, on his little motorcycle, followed behind them along the mountain road.

Jacob's almost hidden smile tugged his cheeks as he navigated toward a shaded glen. This small patch of land watched over by ancient trees and a small waterfall was her favorite place. Peace radiated from the cluster of trees and the demure trickle of water splashing into the glassy pool. Originally, this spot was rather inaccessible. Jacob had cut out a road to make it easier for Hollie to spend time here.

They'd camped for their honeymoon, saving money and dreaming under the stars. Sharing a sleeping bag in the bed of his truck, they made love through the night.

Milo's motorcycle sputtered as they exited the truck. When the motorcycle shut off, a chorus of birdsong replaced the man-made soundtrack. Chattering bugs deepened the natural melody as Hollie unloaded the dogs. Jacob worked quickly to set up a long leash so their three fur babies could not only roam a bit but stay safe and secure.

Jacob hitched the border collie, Ziggy, to the leash, while Bandit, the collie and Lab mix pup, wagged his tail, excited to join his faux-brother.

With deft hands, Jacob added Bandit and Scottie to the run. The pups pranced around as Hollie filled a travel water bowl and set it down.

Milo walked his motorcycle to the side, removing his full-face red helmet that matched his bike. "Wow, look at all that gear securing the pups. In my day, we just tossed them in back and took off. You'd think those were your babies."

Bristling, Hollie struggled to keep the irritation from her voice. "It's a rule here at the ranch—for us and for our guests. Dogs need to be secured for a number of reasons—cats, too."

"Uh-huh," Milo said, swapping his helmet for his camera.

Jacob dropped the tailgate on the truck, a picnic basket and a cooler in the back. "If there's a wreck, the animal could be injured from the force of being loose. Even on a regular outing, they might bolt away when a door is open or window is down. A pet roaming free in a vehicle could also get under the driver's legs and feet, blocking the brakes or gas pedal."

Hollie pulled out a red-and-white-checkered picnic blanket. With a snap, she unfurled the cloth and let it flutter onto the bed of the truck. "We welcome personal pets at the Top Dog Dude Ranch, with a few conditions. Owners must supply all up-to-date vaccination records. Dogs must be kept on a leash, and cats must be in a carrier. Our hope, down the road, is to expand to include boarding services if people want to bring their pets without keeping them in the cabin."

"That's fantastic," Milo said, *snap, snap, snapping* pictures as he talked. "I didn't mean to sound judgy about the dog seat belts."

From somewhere in the trees, Hollie heard the distinctive gobble of a wild turkey. So many animals nestled into the brush on this land. She and Jacob had spent countless hours just listening, so much so she began to discern the critters' distinct voices. She would miss that aspect of ranch life. As much as she wanted to start over and leave the hurt, she knew that this land was a part of her, too.

As if intruding on her musings, Jacob strode past, so close she caught a whiff of his spicy aftershave. Needing space to bolster her resolve, she made her way to the back seat of the truck to pull out the overstuffed picnic basket, ordered from their kitchen. She returned and wordlessly began unloading the array of goodies into the back of the truck with the picnic blanket—apple-cinnamon doughnuts, blueberry scones, raspberry pastry, fresh-picked strawberries with homemade whipped cream, and a carafe of gourmet coffee.

He'd picked her favorites, and she had to admit, she was touched.

And confused.

Jacob adjusted his black Stetson. "No worries. Let's wrap up your photos so my wife and I can have our picnic."

"Absolutely." Milo winked. "I wouldn't want to get in the way of romance."

Hollie stifled a wince. Was that his motive? But to what end? A fling before they split? That seemed cruel to both of them.

Standing by the tailgate, Jacob extended his hand to her, waiting to help her up. She slid her fingers into his warm grasp. Her breath hitched as she leveraged up into the back of the truck.

Milo adjusted settings on his camera while two white-tailed deer moved through the tree line. He shifted and snapped a picture with surprising speed before turning back to them.

"Alright, you two. Jacob, can you feed your wife a strawberry? The light is soft and enchanting back here."

As her husband leaned in, her heart beat faster, attraction and sorrow becoming confused. She pushed herself to process on autopilot as Milo called out more instructions, guiding them through a fake meal, followed by a walk bedside the waterfall for a few more pictures of them with the dogs—a family portrait, he'd called it.

Scottie—cradled in her arms—licked her chin, and real laughter burst from her lips. Jacob's touch on the inside of her wrist sent butterflies rippling through her chest. His thumb stroked gently. His eyes were full of so much light she looked away as she waited for Milo's next direction.

"Alrighty, then," Milo said, backing up a step. "I think we got some top-notch shots. You two are the picture of romance. I'm thoroughly enjoying this assignment. The homey cabin you put me in makes this gig all the sweeter."

"We're glad you're comfortable." Jacob palmed her back with one hand, holding two dog leashes with the other. "Thank you again for your flexibility today."

Milo waved to them before packing away his camera into the motorcycle's black saddlebag. "You two certainly have a full plate. I'll leave you to your picnic and get over to Allegra's bridal brunch."

Hollie threaded her fingers through her pup's fur. "If you have any questions and can't reach us, Ashlynn will be right there to help you. This shower was her doing, and she deserves the credit."

"With the two mothers feuding like crazy, who knows what may happen? But I bet it will be memorable." Milo mounted the bike, strapped on his helmet and sputtered away, leaving her alone with her husband.

All alone.

She watched Jacob's broad shoulders, his strong hands as he checked the three pups on leashes, letting them lounge under the tailgate with a big bowl of water. Muscles rippling, he swung back up onto the truck bed, settling beside her. He pulled out a thermos of coffee and poured her a mug—with two splashes of cream, just as she liked. They knew so much about each other, shared so much history.

Passing over the pale brown java, he grinned. "See, we made it through the photoshoot without a single lip-lock."

"I stand corrected." She curved her hand over his to take the mug. "You didn't have ulterior motives for bringing me out here."

He didn't answer, just gave some sort of "hmm" as he broke a raspberry tart in half and tucked the bite into his mouth.

And suddenly, she didn't want to know if he had a hidden agenda for bringing her here. She just wanted to enjoy this moment. "Thank you for the breakfast and for bringing me here for my favorite doughnuts. It was a lovely thought. I didn't mean to sound ungrateful."

"It's alright. We're both on edge this week."

She cradled the mug in her hands, the warmth seeping in, but not deep enough to chase the chill from her heart. "But I'm the one who fell apart. I was a total sobbing mess on your chest."

"I thought we were going to keep this outing more upbeat." His eyes searching hers, he passed a basket of pastries.

Nodding, giving him a half smile, she chose a flaky blueberry scone. "This place does carry a lot of happy memories."

Jacob popped the last bite of his raspberry pastry into his mouth before dusting powdered sugar off his fingers, wiping his hands along his jeans. "Like camping under the stars."

"Skinny-dipping under the waterfall." The words fell out of her mouth before she could think, and it was too late to call them back. She looked away quickly, her gaze lingering on the way sunlight filtered through the trees.

She missed him, she acknowledged to herself. For so many weeks, she'd shoved aside that thought, fearing she couldn't get through this if she let herself remember any of the good times together. But was that fair to their past?

He skimmed a knuckle down her arm. "We decompressed here more than once."

Once her pulse steadied, she risked a glance back at him and admitted, "The best anniversary gift you ever gave me was widening the path to get here."

The anniversary that fell during her cancer treatments. They'd come here often to escape the weight of chemo. Once her incision from the hysterectomy healed, he'd brought her here to swim under the waterfall.

To heal.

It had been a beautiful night. A thoughtful, emotional act to reclaim her body after the trauma it had been through. Jacob had understood her need to do that. And he'd given her a way to feel whole again, though forever changed.

His throat moved in a slow, emotional bob. "I'd have paved the entire thing if it could have…"

"I know." She rested a hand over his. Too often she got so wrapped up in her pain that she lost sight of his.

But she knew he'd gone through hell, too. Who else would ever understand so well? Tenderness welled up inside her.

Before she could think or reason, she angled forward and pressed her mouth to his.

Chapter Six

Wary of spooking her, Jacob held himself still even though he ached to haul Hollie closer, to deepen the kiss. He wanted to recline her on the truck bed and make love to her in the morning sun.

She dropped her crumbled scone. Then her fingers glided up his face to tunnel in his hair, all the encouragement he needed.

Jacob wrapped his arms around her and drank in the feel of his wife against him. The kiss on the bridge in their wedding garb had whet his appetite in a way he couldn't ignore. The taste of cinnamon on her tongue, the scent of lilac on her skin. She was all the best of his past, and he didn't know how to face a future without her.

And from her response, she wasn't immune to him either, in spite of all the distance she'd put between them since JJ's birth mother took him back.

The thought of their child splashed icy reality onto his passion. He struggled to push down those thoughts, to throw himself into this moment.

But Hollie must have sensed the shift, or at the very least, his break in the connection ended the moment for her as well.

She angled back, her eyes still dazed with desire. "I thought you said we weren't going to do this."

"I said I wouldn't kiss you." He massaged his fingers along the base of her spine, already dreading the moment she would leave his arms. And for how long? "Since *you* kissed *me*, I kept my word."

"Was that your ulterior motive?"

He hesitated, weighing his words. She deserved honesty, but he didn't want to make her run.

"My motive was to help us find a more level place in our relationship before we live under different roofs." He tucked a wayward strand of hair behind her ear, trailing his fingers along her neck.

Angling away just a hint, she scooped up the

basket of raspberry pastries like a barrier between them. "Before we divorce?"

He ignored her question. "We have a lot of good memories. And we have so many successes to celebrate. I don't want those to be overshadowed by the bad."

"I know that." Her lips went tight and she snatched a container to dump the pastries in along with the apple-cinnamon doughnuts. Then she sealed it tight and placed it back in the hamper with exaggerated precision. "As much as I wanted that kiss, I also don't expect that it will wipe away our struggles."

Irritation began to itch up his spine. "Well, *I expect* that we should do better than this."

"I'm not sure I understand. We are wading our way through a divorce trying our best not to hurt each other. I think that's pretty admirable. What are you really trying to say?"

"We've been a part of each other's lives since we were teenagers. I don't have an adult memory that doesn't include you in some way." He swallowed hard. "This place is going to be empty without you."

"Have you considered that the ranch is all that is holding our marriage together?" Her eyes held his, years of pain darkening them as her voice dropped off to a near-tearful whisper. "And if that's the case, then we are just business partners."

The kiss they'd just shared made a lie of that statement. But he wasn't going to press her. He'd gotten her alone. He'd earned a kiss.

Slow and steady would win the day with Hollie now, the same way it had so many years ago. Because he refused to believe she could be right on this. "We're more than just business partners, Hollie. And I hope you see that before you leave."

Freddy wondered how much longer they would have to ride the pony before he could go swimming. Instead, he was stuck waiting in line for his turn.

All the kids on the ponies seemed to be conspiring in some kinda happiness that looked bogus. Phillip, his brother, brought his hands to his face and let out an excited whoop as Freddy adjusted in Freckles's saddle. And of course, that brat Isabella was posing for the camera, pretending to be a lot sweeter than she was as she waited in line ahead of him. His sister, Ivy, was sitting under a shady tree reading a book—she was really smart like that, already reading in kindergarten. Elliot was lying on his stomach, mouth moving.

Probably talking to a beetle or a caterpillar.

Freddy wouldn't have minded the horseback riding, except they did all these pack-tivities that were supposed to help them deal with their *feelings*. If it was so great, why had Isabella still cut in line to get her ride?

Still, some of the stuff they'd done hadn't been half bad. They'd used special safe paint and painted the horses with their hands. He overheard Ms. Shawna talking about how they were doing something called "equine therapy."

He didn't want to be in therapy. There was nothing wrong with him. They said they were all worried because they thought he was trying to run away when he climbed out the bunkhouse window onto the porch. He wouldn't leave his siblings. Ever. But he couldn't confess the truth.

He'd just wanted to go to sleep on the porch and pretend he had his own room again.

At least he didn't have that Mr. O'Brien trying to pretend they were buddies or something. Freddy wasn't stupid. The O'Briens were being paid to let the kids be here. Nobody here really cared about them.

"Next," the old man with a beard called out, then looked down to read his name tag. "Good morning, Freddy. Say hello to Buttercup."

Buttercup? For real? How come he couldn't

have gotten Champ? And no way was he talking to any of the horses. He wasn't Elliot.

Stomping up the mounting block, Freddy looked over enviously at Isabella who flipped her hair beneath her helmet. She was on Dusty. That also sounded better than Buttercup.

Freddy sat down in the saddle and found himself asking, "Where's Mr. O'Brien?"

Why was he asking about him? That didn't make sense.

Mr. Lonnie handed him the rope reins and patted the creamy white pony on her neck. "He and his wife are having breakfast together, just taking a break. There's a lot going on this week, and they're smart to make sure they don't overdo. That's also why they have so many of us in their staff family."

"Staff family?" Buttercup walked lazily around the green grass arena while Mr. Lonnie walked nearby.

"We all work closely together. We love each other like family."

Okay. Whatever.

Freddy looked Mr. Lonnie up and down, cocking his head to the side. "Did anybody ever tell you that your beard is like Santa Claus's?"

"I may have heard that before. And it's not just the beard." He patted his stomach. "It's also all those second helpings of Patsy's famous caramel cake."

Buttercup's speed picked up, and Freddy grabbed the horn of the saddle. This was the first time he'd ever been on a pony or horse. The feeling was odd, like he was slightly off balance with each step Buttercup took.

How did cowboys make this look so easy? He squeezed his legs tighter, trying to anchor himself to the warmth of the horse's sides. Every gasping breath drew in the smell of hay and leather.

Bright sunbeams seemed to punch his eyes as he looked past his brother riding Freckles, who was a white-and-red pony. Freckles and Buttercup, Mr. Lonnie had said, used to be wild ponies from an island in Virginia. They were transported to Top Dog Dude Ranch, and then were "broken" so they could be ridden by annoying kids like Isabella.

Freddy didn't know much about horses, but being broken sounded pretty awful. He understood how lame and unfair it was to be taken far away from home.

His gaze slipped outside this crummy arena to a family of four in the distance—the little boy was walking along a low stone wall, his tennis shoes lighting up each step of the way. Freddy's parents used to take them camping nearly every weekend in the summer. They had a pop-up camper, and his dad had a big truck. They took their canoe, too. Their mom brought her guitar, and she would sing by the campfire while they made s'mores.

Freddy gulped down the thoughts, the taste of chocolate going sour in his memory. He shot a sideways look at Mr. Lonnie. "I'm not an orphan, you know, like these other kids. My parents took jobs with those doctors who go to other countries, and so we had to stay in the group home for a while."

"Doctors Without Borders?" Mr. Lonnie's bushy eyebrows lifted.

"Right. That. Except they are doctors for animals…" The story gained momentum in his mind.

"Veterinarians?"

Freddy scratched beneath Buttercup's mane. He kinda liked the pony. Not as much as Champ, the jet-black pony with a white streak down his face. But still. Maybe Buttercup wasn't so bad after all. "Yep. They're vets. They save magical pets, so they sent us here while they work."

Mr. Lonnie adjusted his Stetson. "Hmm… That's interesting."

Freddy looked down at his name tag. Underneath his name, instead of a home city, it listed the group home. He looked up fast to Lonnie. "They gave me the wrong tag by mistake."

"I'm not worried about that." Mr. Lonnie patted Buttercup's neck. "I just want to make sure you enjoy your pony ride."

Freddy hated when people felt sorry for him. Everybody used to tell him what a lucky little boy he was.

No one said that anymore.

Mr. Lonnie brought Buttercup back around to the beginning of the line and showed him how to swing off. His stomach knotted as his boots hit the dirt with a thud.

Not because the way off the saddle had been scary, though. He scanned the arena and grounds for his siblings, that panic rising in his tummy and chest. He knew it was silly. But he kept thinking they would get split up and not have a chance to say goodbye.

Except Elliot wouldn't have spoken to him anyway unless Freddy turned into a horse or a dog or a cat.

Scanning, he saw Phillip join Ivy under the tree. Then finally—thank goodness—he found his other brother in his straw cowboy hat, walking toward the split rail fence. He was alone.

Of course he was. Elliot was almost always alone now.

Even when he wasn't, it was almost like he was. Elliot had gone somewhere far away—or so it seemed—a place where he could only connect with animals. Elliot leaned on the fence near where a white pony with shaggy red hair and a big belly grazed underneath a really big oak tree.

He missed talking to Elliot. He knew his brother was still in there, but he even missed the way Elliot used to follow him around and do whatever he did.

"Hey, Elliot," Freddy called, walking over, "did you see they're gonna let us go camping in tents while we're here?"

Elliot extended his hand to the pony, pushing out his small arm between the railing. He kept his palm perfectly flat just like Mr. Lonnie had showed them. That way a curious horse or pony didn't think you had a treat and wouldn't accidentally bite one of your fingers.

The pudgy pony didn't even stir. Just continued to eat the light green grass. Elliot's jaw flexed as he looked up at the fence.

With determination, his little brother climbed on the split rail fence to talk to the pony. "Do you like to go camping? I will give you my hot dogs."

See? He knew his brother heard him, so why couldn't he look him in the eyes?

"Um, Elliot, horses eat carrots. Did you know that?" His brother didn't even turn his head, just kept petting the horse and ignoring Freddy. It made him mad. "You're gonna have to start talking to people soon. It's important. They're talking about making you go to a bunch of doctors to find out what's wrong with you."

Elliot leaned on the top part of the fence as the pony looked up from his midday snack. "I'll get you carrots. Will you be my friend?"

Two hoof steps later, the white pony was against the fence within Elliot's reach. His brother's eyes lit up. The sight made Freddy excited to make his brother happy, but it also made him wince a bit. Elliot used to want to be *his* friend, before their parents died, but Freddy told him to bug off. He was really sorry about that now.

Freddy hoisted himself up on the fence, his sweaty hands slipping on the chipping paint. "I told Ms. Shawna that you used to talk to people a lot, but I'm not so sure she believes me. Or maybe she does, and that's bad, too."

Elliot didn't even look at him as he stroked the pony's neck. "Don't be bad. You'll have to go to time-out."

Frustration knocked around inside Freddy. Why couldn't he get through to his brother? "I wonder if it would be better if you could write. Would you write me a note?"

Elliot took the pony by the face and moved his head in a back-and-forth no.

Freddy wanted to shake him. But something told him his brother would run away if he did that. Elliot was like a potato chip these days—really easy to break.

"Would you tell me, though, Elliot? If you were sad?"

Everything went quiet. All he could hear from his brother was shaky breathing as he dropped his hand down to the fence rail. Elliot didn't even talk to the horse. He hopped down off the fence and walked back to the wagon that had brought them over.

Had that been wrong to say? His stomach hurt worse now.

Maybe Elliot really did need equine therapy— or therapy with a doctor. But what if they made him go somewhere else to do that? Once they split them up a little bit, then it would be easier to send them all to different homes. To be a part of different families.

His breakfast pancakes made him feel sorta

sick, like when he ate a whole bag of potato chips. And no matter how hard he tried to be good, to fix things, he couldn't make his family okay again. Times like this, he figured he might as well get as much fun out of this trip as possible. Things couldn't get any worse.

Anger cranked up inside him as he watched Elliot plop down on the wagon. Freddy's stomach flipped again, and he felt tears swell in his eyes. He clenched his fists at his side and wanted to scream.

After a few moments of pushing back all the hurt and tears, he turned back around just in time to see Isabella starting trouble again. Ivy had stopped reading to get back in line.

And that bright-eyed mean girl smiled all fakey as she shoved Ivy out of line. Just like that, blood boiled in his body as he sped over to them.

"Hey, Isabella," he shouted, stalking over to her. He wasn't going to hurt her. His dad was right about not hitting girls. But his dad also always said that he should look out for his sister. That was his job. And thinking about doing that made him forget about his stomach. "You cut in line. My sister is s'posed to ride again."

Isabella looked over at him with a big old grin on her face. But Freddy knew a snake when he saw one.

"Your sister said I could have her next turn on the horse."

Nuh-uh. Not gonna happen.

There were a lot of ways to handle this. He smiled back, waving, walking closer. "That was nice of Ivy."

His sister had tears in her eyes.

Freddy took another step and pretended to trip.

"Look out," he shouted at Isabella.

Her eyes went wide and she backed fast, really fast. Just like he planned. She stepped right into a slick pile of pony poop.

"Fiona and Jayden Rossi, I now pronounce you husband and wife—again," the groom's brother—who also happened to be a pastor—announced.

Hollie's head was still reeling from the picnic with her husband, from his kiss. The tableau of the couple renewing their vows with their two kids looked just like Hollie's dream for her future back at the start of her marriage to Jacob. She smoothed her hands down her floral spring dress, her palms damp.

The couple had chosen to renew their vows on a hillside under a tree, with their children as their "bridesmaid" and "best man." A handful of extended family gathered to watch, each blowing bubbles into the breeze.

Fiona's easy grace was perfectly captured with her upswept, ringleted blond hair as she twirled with her young daughter. Delicate accents of lace on her chest and sleeves made her look enchanting. She leaned forward to kiss Jayden, and he removed his black Stetson, holding her close against his black vest.

The little girl had pinned up her braided pigtails with special ribbons, and the toddler boy jumped around to activate his light-up tennis shoes.

Guests applauded, and others continued to send bubbles skyward. Rainbows reflected in the bigger bubbles as they drifted on a soft spring breeze. Hollie's heart edged toward a precipice, her ability to feel joy and not despondency as fragile as the bubble the toddler sent toward a cluster of thin-limbed trees.

Hollie watched her husband across the field on his cell phone, making calls to the lodge while she made sure everyone had bubbles and pouches of bird seed.

Carefully, Hollie picked her way through a cooing crowd, snippets of conversations drifting over her.

"What precious little ones…"

"…I love that the kids could be part of the celebration."

"Those children are the crown jewels in their love story…"

Quickening her pace, she grasped the edges of her wrap tighter around her. As she angled past a willow line, a familiar young voice drifted on the wind, a voice that didn't belong with this wedding party. She scanned until she found the source…

Freddy, the same child that fled out a window the night before, leaned up against one of the decorative haystacks, his green baseball cap backwards on his head. Dark brown hair stuck out the sides as he rested his hands in the pockets of his stonewashed denim overalls. "Wow, this ranch really is full of magic." He pointed to a couple by the open barn door. "It brought my parents back."

His words tugged at her heart…until she heard Freddy use that as leverage to get a woman's bag of party favor candy. Shaking her head and stifling a smile, Hollie put her hand on his shoulder. "Freddy, you need to come with me."

He sighed, then cast a forlorn look at the sympathetic grandma. "I guess it's time to go back to my mom and dad. I was really hoping they could have some time alone. They stay super busy taking care of my brothers and my sister."

"Freddy," Hollie cautioned softly, "we need to let these people get back to their party."

A woman with long, tumbling silver gray hair waved her manicured hand, costume rings glittering in the sunshine. "He's not bothering me at all, darlin'." Her thick Southern accent added to her almost ethereal charm. "He's absolutely precious."

"Yes, he is," Hollie said. And he was also a handful. "I hope you enjoy the the after-party."

She steered the rascally kid away from the party, catching Jacob's eyes in the distance. Her husband's eyes widened, and he nodded toward Freddy. Funny how some instincts of such a long marriage were tougher to ditch, such as the way they could feel each other's gaze and need for attention. Jacob waved his phone. He would call to alert Shawna. And Hollie would guide him away from the gathering without a scene.

A whole conversation with no words.

They really were good business partners, even though she'd thrown those words at him earlier as if they detracted from their marriage. And that hadn't been fair when she took pride in that part of their relationship, even now. But it hurt that they couldn't figure out how to support one another personally the way they did professionally.

Turning her attention back to the boy at her side, she wished she could steer him toward something that would hold his interest this week.

"Freddy," she said gently, "those people aren't your parents. They're an engaged couple from Mississippi, and they're here to watch their friends renew their vows."

"I know that." He shrugged, stuffing his hands in his pockets. "I was just having fun and getting some of the cool party stuff."

"You shouldn't tell lies."

"It was just a game."

"Do you have something you want to talk to me about?" she asked, drawn to this kid, curious about his story in spite of her resolve to keep her distance.

"Nope." He adjusted his baseball cap. "Is it time for the hayride yet?"

"You'll have to ask Ms. Shawna if you'll be going on the hayride. She might be upset that you ran off again."

He looked down, kicking some dirt. "I get on her nerves."

"It's scary when you're not where you're supposed to be. They're responsible for you, and from everything I can see, they work really hard to keep track of you."

"Yeah, well, I only got to come to the pony rides today because they didn't want to tell my brothers and my sister no. Ivy cried when she thought I couldn't come."

"I can tell you love each other very much." She paused, not sure how far she could push him—and if he would even give her an honest answer. "Why did you tell that lady those other people were your parents?"

Still, this kid compelled her. Maybe it was his acting out that reminded her a little bit of herself at his age. Regardless, she stayed. She listened.

For a moment, Freddy's bravado wavered. His eyes looked glassy. But then he blinked four times, and the pain she thought she was detecting evaporated, replaced by a toothy, mischievous grin.

"I came over to this wedding because I need to hide out." His face scrunched sheepishly. "I'm gonna be in trouble for making Isabella step in poo."

Oh my. Hollie stifled a smile. "I'm sure you didn't mean to."

"Oh, I meant to, alright."

Well, that wasn't what she'd expected. "Why would you do that?"

He just shrugged.

Before she could ask anything more, Jacob strode over to them, putting his cell in the back pocket of his jeans. His head cocked to the side, the brim of his Stetson shading his face from the midday sun. "Is everything okay?"

Hollie patted Freddy lightly on the shoulder. "Our little escape artist here wanted to join the party."

Jacob pulled out his cell phone again and swiped the device to life. "We need to give Shawna a call. She must be frantic."

A grin spread wide across Freddy's face. "Don't worry about that. She doesn't even know I'm gone. She thinks I'm at the lasso class, and the lasso class thinks I'm at goat yoga."

Chapter Seven

An hour later, Jacob slung bales of hay into the back of the wagon. Sure, there were others who could do the work, but he prided himself on rolling up his sleeves when the occasion called for it.

And truth be told, he needed the outlet for his frustration stemming from his messed up life and the very real possibility that his wife could be divorcing him, no matter what he did.

His gaze was drawn to Hollie, like always. Her dress danced in the wind as she approached shoulder to shoulder with Shawna. The two women were in what appeared to be deep, serious conversation judging by the way Hollie's head inclined while Shawna spoke, her hands gesturing in a flurry.

Watercolor florals in shades of twilight blue made Hollie look like a nymph as she approached. And what was it about his wife that made him get downright poetic at times? He'd never figured that out. So he just watched, soaking in the sight of her.

Her dark hair fell in waves, rippling as she walked. The wind drew her gauzy dress until it hugged her gentle curves. His breath hitched at her beauty. But then he saw the worry that pressed Hollie's lips into a tight line.

Shawna's brow furrowed deeply as she tightened her grip on her rainbow clipboard.

Jacob straightened. "Is everything okay?"

"It will be." Shawna placed a hand on Hollie's shoulder as they stopped by the wagon. "I was just thanking Hollie. You've been very understanding. I want you to know we don't take it lightly that Freddy keeps slipping away. I've sent one of our newer counselors back and brought in two more. That additional person will be assigned to Freddy and only Freddy."

Poor kid. That didn't sound like much of a vacation to Jacob, but he appreciated the need for additional eyes on the little rascal. Toying with a loose piece of hay, Jacob pressed the strand between his gloved fingers, the tangy earth smell hanging in the air.

He'd always had a soft spot for kids, especially the ones struggling. "Thank you. We just want him to be safe."

"Freddy needs this place, probably more than any of the other children." Shawna glanced over at the cluster of kids gathered under a tree for story time with the young school librarian dressed up in a fairy costume, reading a book about Sulis Springs.

Lines of concern in Hollie's face etched deeper. He knew she took their mission as seriously as he did. One of the many ways they made a good team. She hitched herself up to sit on the open back of the wagon. "That's why we started this place and why we see it as more than a vacation spot."

Shawna leaned in to say quietly, carefully, "Please do know that even though we're trying to make it work with Freddy staying, there will be consequences for his behavior today."

Jacob dropped the last of the bales into the wagon and tugged off his work gloves. "Just let me know what I can do to support you."

"Thank you. Actually, if you could hold on for a moment, I'll be right back." Shawna straightened, striding over to the group of children gathered on the quilt. She knelt down beside Freddy and whispered something in his ear.

The seven-year-old adjusted his ball cap and stood, dragging his feet as he followed alongside her.

Freddy sheepishly scuffed the toe of his shoe through the dirt. "Mr. and Mrs. O'Brien, I'm really sorry for causing so much trouble. I hope I didn't mess up those people's party."

Hollie squatted in front of him. "Apology accepted. Thank you. I know saying you're sorry isn't always an easy thing to do."

"Freddy," Shawna said. "I need you to look at me and pay attention. Are you listening?"

"Yes, ma'am." Freddy's eyes were bright and full of so much pain for someone so young.

"What you did by wandering off is very dangerous." Shawna fixed him with a no-nonsense gaze. Her voice was soft, but brimming with authority.

His jaw jutted. "But I stayed with the grownups."

"Those adults were also strangers," Shawna continued in a calm, steady voice. "What would you think if your brothers or your sister wandered off like that?"

Freddy shuffled his feet. "Not good."

"That's right. Now, I'm giving you a second

chance, but I need you to understand that this is your last chance. If you wander off again, I'm going to have to send you back to the home for the rest of the vacation."

Jacob's gut knotted in sympathy for the kid. But he knew better than to interfere. Hollie's hand tucked into his, and she squeezed. A jolt of surprise shot through him. Then, just as quickly, she let go. The sense of loss swept over him, too much for the loss of a simple touch. How much worse would it be when she left his sphere for good?

Freddy looked toward the group of children. Concern and panic made his bottom lip wobble. "What about Elliot and Philip and Ivy? Would they have to leave, too?"

"They would stay. It's not fair to punish them for your behavior."

His eyes went wide. "They'll be scared if I'm not here."

Jacob could see now how very tricky it was navigating these disciplinary waters. He didn't want to do something wrong, so he just listened and decided to take his lead form Hollie.

Shawna nodded as she squatted down to his eye level. "What do you think you could do to help make up for the time you took away from the staff today? And last night, too, since they had to stay out late to check on you?"

Freddy scratched his head for a moment. "Maybe I could brush one of their dogs, maybe the one with all that long fur. I've noticed he gets leaves stuck in it sometimes."

Shawna glanced at Hollie and Jacob.

Jacob gave a quick nod. "That would be great, if you could help us get Ziggy ready before the hayride tonight with Mr. Lonnie."

Grinning her thanks, Shawna said, "I think that's a very good idea, Freddy, and really nice of Mr. and Mrs. O'Brien."

Hollie knelt in front of the little boy. "Ziggy does have very long fur and needs brushing all the time."

"Ziggy? That's a cool name." Freddy grinned, walking backward fast. "Come on, come on, come on. I'm ready."

Chuckling, Jacob stuffed his work gloves into his back pocket. "How about you finish story time, and then I'll see you over at the barn?"

Shawna tucked a pen behind her ear, giving Jacob a small wave as she left to join story time, sitting by Freddy's twin brothers. The librarian was passing out animal puppets to all the kids to chime in for an interactive story, and they would keep the puppets after as a party prize. Little Elliot was already talking to the llama puppet on his hand.

What was going on inside that little fella's mind? What would it take to help him rejoin the world around him?

Shaking off the thought, he shifted his attention to his wife. Hollie followed a step behind Freddy, dust from the hay padding her path. His eyes tracked her as she sat on the quilt, her flowing dress settling around her as she took her place beside Freddy. Keeping him safe until the extra help arrived?

That was likely the explanation. Because he could have sworn that up to now, she'd been doing her best to avoid spending time with the kids. Even now, there was a hint of tension in her shoulders. Not that he expected others would notice, but he knew her too well. He could see now that he was wrong to push her about trying adoption again before they'd split.

Maybe that was the answer. If he wanted to make significant inroads into wearing down her resistance to seeing the ways they were good together, he needed to help her in avoiding the heart tug of the children whenever possible.

And make some plans for decidedly adult time.

* * *

Standing on a split rail fence outside the barn, Hollie knew she shouldn't be watching her husband.

But she couldn't pull her gaze away from the sight of Jacob showing Freddy how to brush Ziggy. He was so patient, including Freddy's twin brothers in a seamless manner that didn't call attention to the fact one of the younger boys only spoke to the animals. Shawna stood beside her, scrolling through work emails while waiting for the Hudson children to finish—and for the additional help for Freddy to arrive.

Eliza, one of their newer employees, eager to impress, buzzed behind her, readying horses for Allegra and her family. A saddle slung on her hip, she hoisted the red quilted saddle pad on the back of a white mare. She then made quick work of the black Western saddle with gold embellishments.

Normally, the good tack was reserved for shows and demonstrations. But Hollie thought they'd make regal wedding pictures. She scanned the group and couldn't locate the bride and groom. But she did spot someone she needed to speak with and thank again… Allegra's uncle, who'd sponsored the children's vacation.

Hollie gathered the chiffon pleats of her dress as

wind lazily blew the grass and her dress sleeves. "Where are Allegra and Simon?"

"They wanted a romantic outing away from the dueling relatives," an older gentleman called out. He jabbed a finger in the direction of Allegra and her fiancé, pushing mountain bikes up a trail, backpacks filled to the brim.

"Shawna, this is Mr. Samuel Woodley, Allegra's uncle. He's the gentleman who sponsored the scholarships for the children."

Mr. Woodley wore understated riding gear, nothing in his appearance to clue people in that he was wealthy. Like Forbes 500 loaded. Hollie appreciated his down-to-earth vibe and the way he gave back to the world that had so richly blessed him.

Shawna extended her hand to shake, wind lifting a lock of her pink-streaked hair. "I'm glad we're finally meeting in person after all those phone conversations. Thank you so much for your generous contribution to these children. They'll never forget this experience."

"Absolutely my pleasure." Every word was a well of affection and appreciation. "My wife grew up in a foster family and was later adopted. We have a heart for the good work you do."

His eyes shifted to a young family of three walking by with fishing poles, and his smile widened at the vignette of happiness. The daughter, who looked no older than ten, sang to herself, but snippets of her alto voice carried. "I am the wave and the wave is my heart."

"Well, Mr. Woodley," Hollie said, "we are all truly moved by your donation and hope that the press coverage of this event will inspire others to do the same."

And speaking of which, where was Milo?

Hollie scanned for the photographer and found him kneeling to snap photos of Freddy as he brushed Ziggy—a tableau that cleaved her heart. Jacob calmly explained how to use the different brushes and combs. Freddy carefully worked a snarl out of Ziggy's fur, the four-year-old dog being so patient, occasionally leaning in to the attention.

The twins joined in the activity while their big sister, Ivy, sat with her back against a tree, a book on her knees. Her lips moved as she turned the pages.

Hollie's gaze stayed on the girl, whose braids were half undone, her ribbons trailing down her light blue T-shirt. "She looks young to be reading. Is she small for her age?"

"Actually," Shawna explained, "she's only five years old and very bright. She's only in kindergarten and already on a second-grade reading level.

She reads to get away from the chaos. A good coping strategy, but we want to make sure she still comes out of her shell."

"She certainly looks engrossed in the story..."

Deep laughter echoed, calling Hollie's attention from Ivy. She looked back to Jacob and Freddy. Jacob had stolen Freddy's baseball cap and wore it sideways. Jacob's signature Stetson was half shadowing the young boy's eyes. Laughter continued to echo.

Shawna folded her arms across her chest, leaning closer as her voice dropped to almost a whisper. "You and your husband are good with Freddy. He's not an easy kid to reach. Thank you for giving him the extra attention."

"Jacob and I both love kids. We always wanted a big family, but it wasn't in the cards." She paused to pull in her emotions, then realized her comment might lead the woman to speculate, to push an agenda Hollie couldn't bear to consider. The best way to forestall that? Share a piece of her pain, of her truth. "Our son would have turned one this month."

Shawna touched her arm gently. "Oh no, I'm so sorry. I didn't know you'd lost a child. Seeing all these kids must be so painful for you."

It was. But for so many reasons more than what Shawna thought.

Hollie clenched her hands together, an old habit for when emotions reached too high in her chest and threatened her breath. "I didn't mean to give you the impression he died. He *is* turning one this month." When JJ had first been placed with them, she'd thought his birth date, so close to their anniversary, was a sign that they were meant to be a family. "We're just never going to see him again because his birth mother took him back."

After that, Hollie stopped looking for "signs." She stopped allowing herself to assume the universe was calling out to her with mystical positive signals. This was her life, and she needed to move forward with accepting the hand that had been dealt to her.

Shawna's eyes went wide as she blinked fast. "Uh, I—"

Hollie shook her head. "Please, there's no need to say anything. I hesitated to mention it, given your job. Child services didn't do anything wrong."

Shawna's mouth pulled into a deep, mournful line. "I'm so very sorry."

"There is nothing anyone can say to make this better. Even Jacob and I struggle with how to comfort each other."

During the early miscarriages, they'd turned to each other. Then they doubled down with determination to carry a child to term. They'd been on the same page for so long, but this last grief had broken them. It had been too much.

Now all they had left was their work. As always, it helped ground her, draw her back into the present.

Waving for attention, Phillip called for Shawna, who apologetically excused herself to help settle him and his siblings back at story time now that Ziggy was thoroughly brushed. People like Shawna whose hearts were expanses of compassion and empathy reminded Hollie there was still good in the world. Even when her own world felt tempest-tossed, a collection of uprooted dreams and broken futures.

Despite the comforting sweet smells of feed and the musk of horses, Hollie felt adrift. She swallowed, pushing her pain down as Jacob approached. His keen eyes were full of knowing. Hollie realized he could read her crossed arms and too-still lines.

His face scrunched. She knew a word was forming by the way the left side of his mouth curled. The near memory of Freddy in Jacob's black Stetson dancing with Jacob around Ziggy burned in her mind. A dream of almost, what might have been, what should have been, laid siege to her heart.

"No," she said preemptively as Jacob strode closer.

"No what?" He swept a tuft of Ziggy's fur off his arm.

"No matter how heart-tugging that kid is," she said softly, careful that no one else could overhear, "I'm not reconsidering adoption. I'm moving forward with our plan."

A lump crystallized in her throat. Every word felt like a half betrayal. But her soul couldn't withstand more pain. She needed to erect walls. Fortify her defenses. No matter how much Freddy, his siblings, and Jacob made her want to fling open gates without fear. Hollie had always been a sensible woman, and logic warned her to stay the course she'd planned—to separate and avoid further casualties of her heart.

She just didn't have it in her to feel those hurts.

"I hear you," Jacob said as he stroked Jazzy, a sweet bay Thoroughbred gelding that ambled up to the split rail fence for attention.

"I hope so. I wouldn't want you to misunderstand that kiss earlier." She was suddenly grateful for the presence of the horse. Some distraction from all of the emotions and indecision that had begun to churn acid in her stomach. Jacob's strong, calloused hands traveled to Jazzy's neck. The bay stretched out, enjoying the attention.

"What kiss?" he said with a wink.

"Thank you for the brunch." She toyed with the neckline of her dress. "It was thoughtful."

"No thanks needed," he said. "We've been burning the candle at both ends for a long while. I think it's time we start following our own advice about making room for downtime to recharge."

"That does feel rather hypocritical of us, not to be following the Top Dog mantra of self-care."

Jacob closed the distance between them, a gleam in his eyes. "I have a proposition."

"What would that be?"

He was a heartbeat from her. How easy it would be to reach out and draw comfort from his muscled chest, his pine-and-clove scent.

A slow smile spread across his face. "That whenever possible, we join in the events."

"But we already do. We go riding and we… and we…"

Words receded as she tried to think of something—anything—they did that wasn't work-related. For all of their talk of self-care at Top Dog Dude Ranch, she was finding that she couldn't re-

member the last time either of them had put de-
compression into practice.

"Exactly," Jacob said concisely. "Other than
horseback riding, we work. And even when we're
riding, it's usually to escort guests. We're not true
participants in the Top Dog experience."

She fidgeted with her wedding ring, her left
thumb rubbing back and forth on the bonded band
and engagement ring. "What do you have in mind,
then?"

"We've always been so busy working. Well,"
he said, spreading his arms wide, "everything is
already in place for each of the events—rehearsal
dinners, showers, weddings, receptions. Down to
the letter. For once, let's enjoy the parties."

A laugh sprang from her lips as she pressed the
palm of her right hand to his chest. "Like wedding crashers?"

"Exactly," he said, grinning, a light in his eyes
that rolled years of weight off his shoulders until
he could have been the groom of two decades ago.
"Like wedding crashers."

Could she really do that? Just pretend nothing
was wrong and take part in the Top Dog magic
for the remainder of her time here—her time with
Jacob? It was an alluring proposition, no doubt.

And after losing so much, she decided it was

time to take something for herself, even if it was just a little time to play with her husband.

The sound of bagpipes split the evening air as the bride and groom sealed their vows with a kiss. Lights twinkled overhead, draped along the sprawling trees.

Jacob applauded, all too aware of his beautiful wife cheering beside him. Relaxed and smiling. A Scottish-themed ceremony was just the ticket for launching his campaign to romance his wife with their wedding crashers plan.

Jacob couldn't remember when he'd last worn his kilt just for fun, rather than as part of some Top Dog Dude Ranch event or Halloween—Hollie's favorite holiday. But crashing this Scottish-themed wedding offered the perfect opportunity. Hollie was a vision beside him in a floor-length tartan gown in the O'Brien plaid of green and blue.

A photo booth had been set up with Scottie for guests to "smooch a pooch." Baskets with heather sachets for the guests were placed behind the rows of plaid-draped seats.

Hollie smoothed her strapless green and blue tartan gown. "This wedding came together better than I expected. I was worried how the colors would blend with red roses to match the plaid, but hints of heather mixed in. The white heather, instead of purple."

Her hand lifted to touch her upswept hair, the fancy twist sporting a hint of traditional lavender-colored heather.

Jacob nodded, his hand resting on his silver sporran. When they were newlyweds, Hollie had scrimped and saved for their first anniversary gift. She had a custom-made sporran with the Queen of the Forest etched in the real silver. The doe's head was flanked by an oak tree, a symbol of strength, and a Scottish thistle to honor his family's immigration and settlement.

His fingers traced the etchings, love filling his heart at the memory. "The new landscaper has a great eye."

And since Charlotte also had a skill for floral arrangements, it had been a great money saver not having to contract out that portion any longer.

"She's a dream to have on staff. I give her full credit for making the bride's wishes blend so tastefully." Hollie drew in a deep breath, the delicate peaks of her shoulders going rigid with tension.

Jacob could practically feel her compulsion to let the job take hold of her body.

Enough of talking shop. He had a mission tonight. "And there it is. The word *work*. We agreed this was going to be about joining the party."

From the stage, a tenor began to sing. A tin whistle twined with the singer's voice.

"One two three. My bonnie lass!" the singer called, keeping time by clapping his hands while a fiddle, guitar and drums quickened the tempo.

Whoops and cheers erupted, the dance floor filling with couples. As the clapping from the band and crowd intensified, Jacob swept Hollie toward the planked expanse. He didn't give her a chance to protest. And, thankfully, she followed his lead.

As he spun her, they joined the chorus of voices singing. The crowd clapped in time with the singer. Hollie laughed as they danced to the Scottish reel. The sound of her joy, the feel of her in his arms, sent an answering happiness through him.

Along with a sizzle of desire to dance her off into the woods, just the two of them. But he knew if he did that, the ease of the moment would be lost. So he resolved to savor the now.

Waiters in kilts carried trays of appetizers—salmon canapés, tiny haggis and oatcakes. They also circulated with champagne and shot glasses of whiskey.

Clusters of guests gathered around the elaborate Scottish brandy fruitcake on the whiskey barrel. Other guests joined the lively dance. Energy spiked as the groom in a red tartan kilt with a jet-black sporran clapped his hands, circling his bride who was dressed in a gauzy white dress, a piece of tartan trailing from her waist over the back of her dress. Seeing their love warmed Jacob's heart as he danced with Hollie.

Applause thundered as the band bowed at the end of the reel. The singer's brogue was strong as he dedicated the next song to lovers old and new.

Hollie nestled deeper into Jacob's arms, swaying to the soulful fiddle. The woman who had played the tin whistle approached the microphone at center stage, deepening the soulful timbre. Hollie hummed lightly under her breath, every brush of her body sweeter than the one before.

Her lilac scent mixed with the oaky whiskey as she spoke. "This brings back memories of the year we celebrated our anniversary with a trip to Scotland."

Jacob whispered in her ear as their bodies melted into each other. "It took me six months to convince you we could afford it."

"Jacob, we couldn't afford it." She tipped her face to his. "You gave private riding lessons to pay for it."

Surprise pulsed through him. "I didn't know you found out about that."

Blue eyes as wild as Scotland's skies looked up at him. She offered a sheepish grin. "I didn't want to hurt your pride. You were so excited to make that trip happen for us."

How many times had she tried to cushion the blow for him? During her cancer battle, he'd seen the pain etched in her face, but she'd always downplayed the suffering. He'd had to find the details through internet searches and pressing the doctor. But what about the signs he'd missed?

As much as he wanted to ask her now, to press her, he'd also promised her this time together was about lighthearted fun. And if he intended to make progress with her, he needed to keep his word. He couldn't risk spooking her.

Hollie's cheek brushed against his. "How did it go with Freddy brushing Ziggy? It looked like he had fun."

"The kid was surprisingly careful, his brothers, too." Jacob had learned long ago to gauge a person's merit by how they treated animals. "I was expecting to have to caution them more, but they were extremely gentle about working out the knots."

Shaking her head, Hollie exhaled hard. "I'm not changing my mind about adoption."

His gut clenched. He did not want to go down this path again tonight, to risk ruining this wary peace. "Hollie," he said gently. "You already said that earlier. And I heard you. And if you recall, I wasn't the one who arranged for these children to come to the ranch."

"But you're good with kids. You always wanted them." She stopped dancing, facing him as the guests moved around them.

"So did you," he reminded her.

"But I can't have them. You can—"

"Stop. I'm not discussing it." He pressed his fingers to her lips. He searched for words that would disperse the tension crackling between them, to stop her from circling back to this same topic again and again. "This conversation has gone way outside the realm of our pact for fun and light-hearted."

The band launched into another reel, just the excuse he needed. Before she could wind up another argument, he clasped her hands in his and swung her into step with the beat. As he took in the flush of her cheeks, the flash in her eyes, a wave of nostalgia went through him, so powerful he questioned the wisdom of his wedding crashers plan.

Because there was a very real chance he could get hurt again.

Chapter Eight

What was wrong with Jacob?

Hollie stared at her husband's back as he rode Goliath, leading a couple dozen guests on the ultimate dude ranch adventure. Kendric and Natalie and their wedding party wanted an extended trail ride.

Most days, Hollie would have enjoyed the chance to get back to nature with time in the saddle. Especially on days she got to ride Trickster. Normally, Trickster had an ineffable way of re-centering Hollie, but even the liver chestnut's steady gait and even temperament couldn't help her this morning.

She was so very confused and frustrated, she was about to crawl out of her skin.

Hollie had been wary of his wedding crashers idea, nervous that he would use it as an excuse to push an agenda. But he hadn't made a move on her during what turned out to be a five-day series of platonic dates woven through an all-business workweek.

Did that mean he'd resigned himself to their split and a new way of interacting? That's what she'd wanted, of course.

So why did everything feel so off between them?

Trickster stepped carefully into the bed of the shallow stream. Water splashed beyond her horse's white stockings, reaching Hollie's midcalf. A cloudless sky and relentless sun made the water a welcome relief.

She glanced to her right, where the stream widened and deepened. Childish squeals of laughter carried on the gentle breeze while kids waded into the stream, their small arms sporting mint and pink floaties. Hollie felt a fleeting pull toward joy as a wiry boy hoisted himself up onto an innertube, a triumphant grin spreading across his face.

Shawna had been true to her word. Freddy

hadn't pulled off another escape. He'd tried, but he hadn't succeeded. By the second day of extra chaperoning, he'd settled in to enjoy the trip along with the other children.

Everyone was happy—the children, the wedding parties. She should be celebrating the successes. In another couple of weeks, she would be packing up to move to the new location outside of Nashville.

She would be…alone.

Which was the opposite of the future she glimpsed before her. Kendric and Natalie's connection was palpable, humming with hope and love. She swore she could feel the strength of their bond in every sidelong glance the couple exchanged. Their wedding party filed along on horseback, sporting their gifts from Kendric and Natalie—Stetsons and new belts with their initials in the buckles.

Hips rolling with Trickster's motion, Hollie recalled the gifts she'd given her bridesmaids. She and Jacob had taken their friends out for a night of pool and darts, the evening as relaxed and simple as their whole wedding had been. Back then, they'd agreed on so many things, including the kind of ceremony they'd wanted.

Adjusting the reins in her hand, Hollie did her

best to refocus as they reached the other side of the shallow stream. Trickster moved through the soft spring grass, ears attentive. "So, Natalie, how long have you two been dating? How did you meet?"

Natalie slowed Foxtrot to keep pace with Hollie. "We've been together for three years."

Kendric maneuvered Nutmeg so that the Thoroughbred was in line with his fiancée. He grinned roguishly. "We met at book club."

"Book club?" Jacob glanced back over his shoulder. "I would have thought you met at riding lessons."

Shrugging, Kendric shot a glance Hollie's way. "I was new to the area and wanted to meet people—"

A groomsman in the back of the pack chuckled. "To meet women, you mean."

"Sure," Kendric answered unabashedly. "So I joined a book club at the library."

Natalie grinned at Hollie before falling into the line. "We read romance novels."

"Well," Jacob said, scrubbing a hand along his stubbled jaw. "That's a unique approach, and one we haven't heard from any of our guests in twenty years of business."

"She likes cowboys." Kendric stroked a finger

along the brim of his hat. "Lucky for me, I happened to have grown up on a farm."

A fallen log ahead narrowed the path, steering them into traveling single file for a moment, and Jacob led the way. Hollie applied slight pressure to Trickster with her calves. The liver chestnut's pace quickened as she followed behind Jacob.

Natalie made a swooning gesture, fanning her face. "He speaks that sexy cowboy lingo."

"This truly was the perfect fit for the two of you to get married." No doubt, the cowboy persona was alluring on a guy. Except Hollie only had eyes for Jacob. She couldn't help but think back to seeing him for the first time as he strode into her father's ice-cream shop, all full of swagger and charm. His ranch roots had shone through and mesmerized her.

Pausing her horse, Natalie leaned forward and rested her arm on the saddle horn. "I was married before—I'm divorced." A shadow crossed her face. "I already did the big wedding then. This time, I wanted to do a destination wedding."

Kendric nodded. "As do I. We told our families and let them know they were welcome to attend, but we were planning everything."

"And no fuss," Natalie rushed to say. "No drama. Right, my love?"

"Amen to that." Kendric held the reins lightly, maneuvering Nutmeg over a decomposing log.

Natalie rode up alongside Hollie. "What about your wedding?"

Her mind skimmed back, not to the day they were married, but the afternoon he walked in on her wearing the gown—then not wearing the gown. "We were young. It was simple, all put together on a shoestring budget. I bought the dress at a secondhand store that took donations for charities..."

As her voice drifted off, Jacob picked up the thread, the quiet of the forest making it easy to be heard. "Our families and a few friends were there. We had each other. I know it sounds ironic that now we throw these big extravagant events for others when that's not what we chose for ourselves. Hollie can probably explain the rationale better than I can."

"Even if we'd had an unlimited budget," she mused, "I think our day would have looked the same. We feel it's about personalizing the event, making it your special time, however that takes shape. The event should be a reflection of the couple."

Natalie sighed. "Sounds magical. Like this place."

Was it?

Not for the first time, Hollie wondered what exactly made the magic ingredients necessary for a lasting bond. She believed in the Top Dog Dude Ranch mission to bring their guests connections and healings through their time there.

Yet she didn't have the answer to that any more than she understood what had made Jacob pull away over the past few days. However, she absolutely knew they couldn't end things on this note— polite strangers—when they got together outside of business.

Once they were alone, she would get to the bottom of whatever game Jacob was playing.

"Is everyone ready to play the game?" Jacob held up his tablet, ready to send the instructions for the outdoor scavenger hunt.

Cheers rippled through the crowd of nearly a hundred adults gathered in the courtyard. His gaze gravitated to Hollie standing on the lodge steps, looking quietly elegant and entirely alluring in jeans and a long-sleeved teal tee. She passed out flashlights and glow stick necklaces.

Yes, he had pulled back from Hollie after the Scottish-themed wedding, and he knew she'd noticed. He still wanted her to stay, but he had to maintain his objectivity and keep his cool while he went about it.

The risk of losing her again if he put himself out there to win her back—he could hardly contemplate how much that would wreck him. He needed a measured approach. A way to make her see they could be good together without savaging his heart again. He just had to figure out the right timing for his next move.

His attention shifted to the throng of partiers in front of him. The children's scavenger hunt was in the barn, supervised by staff—alphabet-based, finding something that started with each letter. Then they would have a camping sleepover with tents in the barns.

This way, the adults could stay out as late as they wished. As the teams broke off, preparing themselves for the activity, he could sense the thrum of excitement in the air.

This had long been a fan-favorite Top Dog activity.

Hollie always took great care in making the list for this type of event, choosing items that would have special significance to the guests. Over the decades, she taught them how to find joy and treasures all around them, usually in the most unexpected places. Snippets of conversation swelled from the guests as they decided which item to hunt for first…

A lady who'd arrived yesterday—Allegra's cousin—excitedly read out, "Take a selfie with a goat and a dog—"

Kendric and Natalie's wedding party clapped, and some of the groomsmen started to sing out their favorites. "Stand on a split rail fence—"

"Video your team singing the theme song to a television show, in front of the Sulis Spring cave—"

"Make a TikTok with a horse—"

Hollie had outdone herself.

This would give Milo plenty of material to add to his feature. The first installment in the paper had been picked up at news outlets across Tennessee.

Ashlynn, Lonnie and Patsy were already parked at picnic tables around a large firepit, the stations positioned outside the lodge so that each guest had an equal chance to log in and verify their results once they completed the list. Hollie's gaze tracked to his. Lingered thoughtfully.

Not for the first time this week, he had the feeling she was on to him—that he'd chickened out partway through his plan to win her back. No doubt she'd felt the shift in his attention, and he wasn't sure what to say if she called him out on it.

Maybe Lonnie would have some words of advice.

Jacob strode over to Lonnie's table and dropped into the seat across from him. "Do you have a minute?"

"Sure, Boss." Lonnie held his Pomeranian—Waylon—in his lap. A lunch box was open on the table, a thermos and snacks inside. "It'll be a while before anyone comes up to verify their hunt results. Would you like a carrot? I'm watching my cholesterol."

"Thanks, but I'm good." Jacob drummed his fingers on the picnic table absently. "I appreciate you and Patsy working tonight. I realize tomorrow's a big day for you with the vows renewal."

"It's a simple ceremony. And you've been more than understanding in giving us time off even though you're going to be neck-deep in events." Lonnie smoothed Waylon's puffy fur and ignored the carrots. "What's on your mind? You haven't seemed all that festive the past few days."

Jacob scrubbed the back of his neck. "I hope the guests haven't noticed."

"I doubt it." Lonnie scratched Waylon between

the ears. "I just know you. So, I'll say again, what's on your mind?"

The words didn't come easy. He had to pry them loose.

"Hollie and I aren't doing so well." That was sure the understatement of the century. But he was hesitant to tell everything. Doing so would make it…real. He settled for a partial truth. "Hollie will be using the time in Nashville to give us some space to sort things out."

"I'm sorry to hear that." A small beat of silence unfurled despite the assembly of guests. Lonnie nodded at him, his eyes gentle. "But I'm also not surprised. You two have been through a lot. It would be more surprising if you hadn't struggled from all the loss."

"I wish it was that simple."

"Life rarely is. And since you opened the door on this discussion, I have a bit of advice to offer." He pushed aside the lunch box, his gaze laser-focused. "I know we talk a lot about the magic at the Top Dog Dude Ranch, but there's more to this place than some mystical element. You've built a program with a firm foundation in techniques that help people cope, that help them heal."

And Jacob was proud of that, too. But it wasn't easy to take his own advice. Besides, he and Hollie had been through crisis after crisis. "I think our troubles are beyond the help of goat yoga or a drum circle."

"That's my point. Early on in our marriage, Patsy and I faced some significant challenges. I had a drinking problem, and I blew through all our money." He held up a hand. "I know those are things I brought on myself, while you and Hollie did nothing to bring on the trials you've faced. But what I do know is that we needed help, professional help, to get us through."

"Counseling," Jacob said softly, remembering other times the idea had come up, only to be discarded.

It had never seemed like the right time, or else they'd had a different plan to handle a problem. But maybe now it was time to reconsider.

"Yes, counseling." Lonnie paused while the words settled in the air between them. Waylon rested a furry paw on Lonnie's wrist. "Thank God, I said yes when Patsy laid down the ultimatum."

Jacob scrubbed a hand over his chest, a spot with a permanent ache these past months. "Thank you for sharing that. You've given me a lot to think about. I appreciate it."

Jacob toyed with the brim of his Stetson before rising. He needed clear air, the winking of stars and planets overhead, and the scavenger hunt game would continue well into the evening. He could afford some time away. Besides, walks on his land often helped him make sense of the world. He started out on the moonlit path, away from the hum of the crowd. Owls sounded in the thick wooded area.

Patsy and Lonnie would be renewing their vows tomorrow, and Jacob didn't want to risk creating any kind of upheaval before then. But the second the ceremony was finished, he and Hollie needed to have a talk. Maybe even test the waters and see if she would be open to therapy.

He intended to spell out, in logical terms, his plan to make the most of what they had left. To show her that they could be together—without risking their hearts.

Hollie's heart was in her throat.

There was so much love at Patsy and Lonnie's vows renewal, the air in the tiny old church hummed with it.

Sun from the skylights in the high-ceilinged chapel washed over the reclaimed wood. Raise the Woof sang old country classic tunes, including ones by their favorite artists—Patsy Cline and Waylon Jennings. Guests dabbed the corners of eyes, clapped and whistled as Lonnie held up Patsy's lace-enveloped arm as they walked down the aisle. Patsy's silver hair was swept upward and held by a pearl comb, the same one she'd worn all of those decades ago.

Hollie watched as the couple walked shoulder to shoulder toward the church door, out into the bright spring sunshine. Silhouetted in the arched doorway, Lonnie leaned in to kiss his wife's cheek. The pews of the rustic log cabin chapel began to empty. Hollie and Jacob entered a living river of excitement, mingling with the many generations of their dear friends and family.

Digging deep to support her friends, Hollie plastered a smile on her face as they maneuvered through the press of people who began to form a line to greet Lonnie and Patsy. Old friends called and waved to Hollie and her husband as they made their way to the door. Jacob's heavy boot falls echoed in the small chapel as promises of recon-nection tore at her.

Lonnie and Patsy's children and grandchildren bustled behind them, all curls and giggles. The close-knit family was a testament to Patsy and Lonnie.

Hollie had wanted that for her life with Jacob, so very much.

With JJ, she'd really thought their dream was coming true. The birth mother had been so certain in their meetings. They'd even met the birth father. The couple were high school sweethearts. They'd had a summer fling before parting ways to go to different universities. Both wanted to continue their education, and neither felt capable to juggling the demands of school, work and parenting.

They'd been emotional, but resolute.

Or so it seemed.

Only a few short months after JJ had been placed with them, the biological grandparents had stepped in with plans. The teens could move back home and enroll in the community college, and the grandparents would help with childcare.

The birth parents had gotten married the next day and had taken their infant son back.

The grief had been gut-wrenching, beyond imagining.

Their lawyer had said they could try to fight it, but the odds were that they would lose. Delaying would only make things tougher for JJ—for Ethan, as he was called now.

Did their son even remember what he'd once been called? Did he remember them?

That thought hurt worst of all.

She blinked, pulling her attention back to the moment before the past swallowed her whole. Lonnie and Patsy's vows renewal was the smallest wedding event scheduled during this extravaganza, but Hollie couldn't help but feel the ceremony was the most magical so far.

Simple and elegant. No extra bells and whistles. Just family and love.

She touched Jacob's arm as he stood beside her, looking heart-stoppingly handsome in a dark blue suit. "Are you okay?" she whispered. "You've been pretty quiet the past few days."

"I apologize." He pulled a smile, the one he used for events at work. "I promise to try harder to be a good wedding crasher."

"You don't have to pretend with me." She squeezed his arm, concern running deeper.

"And you don't have to take care of me."

His words hurt, startling her like a splash of cold water. And confirmed all the more that something was most definitely off with Jacob. She would have pressed, but the line moved, and they were next up to talk to Lonnie and Patsy at the door. The last thing she wanted was to taint their day by letting her worries show.

Hollie hugged Patsy. "Congratulations, dear friend. You look lovely."

Patsy toyed with her little bouquet of pink peonies, a smile lighting her eyes. "Thank you for making it even better than our first ceremony."

Lonnie's arm stretched around Patsy, pulling her close to his chest, all spiffed up in a blue suit. He kissed her forehead. "Well, it was a stressful day for sure back then. Your dad didn't like me one bit."

Patsy winked, snuggling closer. "He came around."

Lonnie squeezed his bride's shoulder as his bright, warm eyes met Hollie's gaze. "He said I wasn't good enough for her. He was right about that. He also said we would never last."

Smoothing a hand over his tie, Patsy gazed up at her husband, her gaze holding his. "We sure showed him."

Lonnie smiled back at her, his eyes full of love. He clasped her hand against his chest. His smile faded, and his hand clenched tighter around Patsy's.

His features went still. Unnaturally frozen for a moment. Concern spiked through Hollie at the same time Patsy frowned.

"Lonnie?" Jacob moved toward the older man, reaching for his shoulder.

Lonnie's face went pale and he sank back against the wall. "Patsy, I think I'm having a heart attack."

Chapter Nine

Medical settings still made Jacob twitchy.

He did what was necessary with regular check-ups for himself, Hollie—and JJ. But it never went away, this tight-chested feeling. The year of Hollie's cancer had brought them here far too often, and every time he'd walked through the doors, he'd had to battle a fear of one day leaving without her.

That time had left a mark.

Today, sitting waiting for news about Lonnie, Jacob had tried all the grounding techniques they taught their guests, using his five senses to catalog his surroundings. But it was tough to push through during the endless hours, desperate for the doctor to update them on Lonnie's condition.

While waiting to find out if his friend was still alive.

As the PA. system droned on with pages for different doctors and nurses, Jacob paced the length of the small waiting area, restless. Above the nurses' check-in desk, the circle of fluorescent lights hummed.

With every step, he inhaled the bitter, antiseptic air. It stung with the reminder of too many memories. Too much fear.

He stuffed his hands in his jacket pockets as he walked across the maroon carpet. If only he could be like Hollie, who was sitting so calmly with Patsy, quietly offering support while Patsy's kids went to the cafeteria for a quick bite to eat.

But he figured better to keep to himself rather than add stress to the others' already heavy load. Lonnie was more than a friend, and more like a mentor. Almost like a dad to him, especially since he didn't see his own dad often.

His parents had retired in Arizona, stating they could embrace the next stage of life now that their son was settled with a purpose, turning the family land into something meaningful. His siblings were married with huge families of their own.

During Hollie's cancer battle, everyone had voiced their support and love, but still he'd been alone. They'd all said to call if they were needed, leaving the invitation vague. He didn't call.

Over time, the people of the Top Dog Dude Ranch had become his family. The kind of family who showed up. Who cared what happened to him on a day-to-day basis. He'd sifted through the hurt of having to split up his extended "family" in this divorce, and he hadn't liked the idea of it one bit. But he hadn't even considered losing a member in such a permanent way.

Lonnie had to be okay. There was no other acceptable answer.

Needing to do something other than think about how very pale Lonnie had looked when he collapsed, Jacob perused the items in the vending machine. Hollie's voice twined around him as she shared stories about Lonnie to keep Patsy's spirits up.

"Remember the year he played Santa Claus and the horse tried to eat his beard?" she reminisced. "He sweet-talked that horse into letting go. I still don't know how."

Hollie's calm, steady demeanor rocked him. Her ability to offer light to others had always attracted him, and was part of how he knew he wanted to have kids with her. Jacob's breath tightened, and he shoved that knowledge away, trying to become very interested in the dimly lit vending machine's popcorn variety.

Jacob risked a side glance to where his wife sat with Patsy. Hollie had her arm around the older woman's shoulders. Patsy's wedding gown was wrinkled now. Her bouquet rested on top of her purse with heart-tugging care.

Tissues mangled in her hands, Patsy nodded. "He said he didn't want to destroy the magic for the children."

Jacob's stomach churned, a physical manifestation of his nerves. He walked by the check-in desk and waved his hand under the hand sanitizer dispenser. Rubbing his hands together, he started to make his way back to the women.

Hollie's blue eyes flicked to him before returning to Patsy. "And then there was the time he brought Waylon along for that couples' massage, and that little mischievous pup stole the towel right off of Nina Archer."

Lonnie always had been a softie. Little Waylon ran the house.

Patsy sat up straight, her shoulders tense. She started to reach down for her leather fringe purse to find her phone. "Who's feeding Waylon? It's past his dinnertime—"

Hollie rested a hand on her arm. "I've already messaged Ashlynn. She said she's happy to keep Waylon for however long you need. Don't worry about him, Patsy."

"I'm trying," Patsy said, twisting the tissue in her hands. "I can't believe I didn't think about Waylon before now."

"You were focused on Lonnie," Hollie said. "That's completely understandable. The grandchildren are fine, and Waylon is fine. Now, could I get anyone some coffee?"

"Yes, please," Patsy said. "Two sugars and a spoon of creamer."

"Um," Jacob interjected quickly. "How about I get it?" No way was he passing up an excuse to get out of this waiting room without letting Patsy down.

Hollie shot to her feet, arms reaching over her head. "I'll go. I really need to stretch my legs. I'll get some java for you, too."

Well, so much for getting away.

No escape now.

Rubbing a hand on the back of his neck, Jacob dropped into a seat beside Patsy and searched for something to say. Boot tapping against the sterile tile floor, he blurted out the first thought that flashed in his mind. "He's going to be okay."

Really? That was the best he could do? If someone had said that to him during Hollie's cancer battle, he would have seethed inwardly.

Maybe even outwardly, too.

Smiling softly, Patsy patted his hand and said, "Thanks for trying. You were always so upbeat during Hollie's treatment."

He hadn't felt that way on the inside, but for his wife, he'd worked not to let his guard down. He'd needed to be strong. And he should tap into that old well of strength for Patsy now.

Jacob took Patsy's hand, holding it tight. "I'm here for you, whatever you and Lonnie need."

And he would be. Except when they moved, they would turn to Hollie. He wanted them to have support. He just wanted to be a part of the picture.

Today had affirmed more than ever how he needed to tread warily, keeping guard over his heart so his life didn't implode again.

Hollie had to battle hard not to expect the worst anytime a person went to the hospital. But hearing Lonnie had only had a minor heart attack went a long way in helping ease her back from that cliff of negative thinking. He would stay in the hospital for observation, and the doctors would discuss the possibility of a stent.

Overall, though, the prognosis was so much better than they'd feared.

Her stomach had been on fire with worry. Now, waiting in the drive-through at her favorite burger joint, she was starving.

Milkshake-shaped neon lights blinked as Jacob navigated the truck to the menu of Mike's Place. From the truck, Hollie watched a vignette of this still small town unfold. A black sports car parked across the lot, a young couple practically leaping from a coupe and heading into the dining area. Mike's Place had been here for over sixty years. The prices had stayed relatively low because it was a family-run operation.

Jimmy, Mike's grandson who ran the burger joint these days, was straightening up the chairs left in disarray by the window. The older Hollie became, the more she understood such small consistencies like the straightening of chairs could blossom into mundane miracles. The simple things in life, those mattered, collectively restoring order to the world.

Jacob rolled down the truck window, arm leaning on the frame as he exchanged a quick greeting with the cashier, then began to order into the speaker. "We'll take a chili cheese dog, two double cheeseburgers—one of those all the way, the other with no tomatoes. A large order of onion rings. And a regular order of sweet potato fries. Two chocolate milkshakes."

He'd remembered her favorites. Such a simple thing, but it touched her heart. How many, many things they knew about one another. The way they took their coffee. The temperature they liked their thermostat—warmer in the daytime, cooler at night.

She knew Jacob sometimes forgot to take his socks off before bed. He knew she had a secret fear of mice, and that's why she always had a cat. Would anyone ever know her so well as this man?

Sometimes the thought of their impending split was so painful it took her breath away.

So instead, she breathed in the scent of grilling burgers drifting on the night breeze. She would focus on the moment. This meal together after fearing Lonnie would die. "I'm proud of the menu we've put together, but man, sometimes it's nice to get good old-fashioned carry-out."

Jacob slanted a look at her, the dashboard glow illuminating the angles of his handsome face. "I'd have cooked for you, darlin', if you asked."

"We're both so tired most days, I would hate

to ask." She already carried such guilt for all he'd given up for her. Quirking her head to the side while the satellite radio played a slow country song, she offered a tight-lipped smile. "Thank you, though. This is a treat."

"You were always so easy to make happy." His eyebrows pinching together, he eased the truck forward in the takeout line. "You should have made me try harder."

What in the world could he mean by that? Without thinking, she touched his forearm, catching his dark gaze in the subdued light. "You already try so hard to take care of everyone, it breaks my heart for you."

When she saw the furrows in his forehead deepen, she knew this line of conversation would just lead them in circles, frustrated and unresolved. She wasn't letting that happen. Not tonight.

"Jacob, stop whatever it is you're mulling over, and let's quit talking about all this serious stuff. We should just enjoy our burgers. If you're nice, I'll even share my onion rings."

"Wow, that's a huge commitment, Mrs. O'Brien. I know how much you love your onion rings," he said with a wink, before turning his attention to pulling up to the drive-through window to get their food.

A teenager with slicked-black hair and braces

smiled as she handed over the thick white-and-orange paper bags. She had folded the top of the bag, half obscuring the logo of a fat burger with a milkshake.

Handing his card to the cashier, Jacob opened the fast food bag. And he even double-checked that they'd included her onion rings. He pulled out one and popped it into her mouth, his fingers lingering for a moment on her lips, teasing a memory to life.

During her cancer treatment, on the days she felt like eating, she was ravenous. And if that rare occasion included an ability to tolerate fried foods? She was downright possessive of her meal. One time he'd reached for one of her onion rings, and she'd smacked his hand playfully.

Cancer was everything she'd feared and nothing like she'd imagined. Who could imagine it, even when they'd seen a loved one go through the battle? Her mom had died of cancer shortly after her wedding, and still Hollie had felt woefully unprepared for all she'd faced.

And then they'd learned she needed a hysterectomy, that she would lose her ovaries, too. Jacob had told her all that mattered was keeping her alive. That didn't stop her from grieving over the death of a dream.

As she chewed through the onion ring, she realized…

Why did all conversation seem to remind her of cancer or JJ? So much so it felt all roads of communication between them led to pain.

As if of its own volition, her hand drifted to her stomach, to her scars from a stillbirth by cesarean, then later incisions from cancer surgeries and her hysterectomy. Physical reminders of all she endured, all the visions of her future that could never materialize. Phantom pain iced her stomach, catapulting memories of their trials and struggles to the forefront of her mind. Her hands clenched around the paper sack.

There had been a time when she and Jacob had comforted each other, in the early miscarriages. Then they'd gone through a time doubling down with determination to carry a child to term. A dream that also failed. All frozen eggs had been used during fertility treatments.

Then hope had dared tease them with the promise of a newborn to adopt. A baby boy who'd snuggled so deeply into their hearts, losing him had destroyed them both. Their pain was so deep, the wounds so debilitating, they had nothing left to offer each other. Even looking at Jacob, she saw all those losses. And she could sense the same flinch in him when he saw her. There was just too much pain between them.

Now all that was left was go through the motions of peddling a magic she no longer believed was real.

Some days took the stuffing right out of a person.

Parked in a patio lounger in the private garden outside his and Hollie's two suites, Jacob divvied up the contents of the bags from the burger joint. He set up their meal on the table between the two chairs, a fire crackling low in the firepit—a smaller replica of the massive firepit outside the front of the lodge. Sparks crackled and floated skyward.

He was grateful to see this day coming to a close without the worst-case scenario playing out. Now that the adrenaline had waned, he was dog-tired. He'd shrugged out of his suit coat and ditched the tie rather than wait another minute to chill and eat.

The French doors from their quarters opened, and Hollie crossed quietly to him. She still wore the silky dress from attending the wedding, but she'd ditched her heels and loosened her hair. She carried two water bottles, with Ziggy, Scottie and Bandit trailing after her.

She passed his drink, then scooted Pippa to the side to make room. The groggy feline protested, pushing back against her hand before finally relenting to curl up the end of the recliner into a tight ball of fur.

Rolling her eyes and half grinning, Hollie took her seat, sitting cross-legged to accommodate space for the cat. She scooped up her burger and took a bite, followed by a soft moan of pleasure. "This reminds me of our early days dating when we used to have picnics and play truth or dare."

Jacob fanned out his sweet potato fries on one of the bags. "You always did like picnics."

"You always liked truth or dare." Their easy laughter twined as if drawn by familiarity. "Remember the time I asked where was a place you'd never made love before?"

"I recall being confused since you should already know the answer to that." And then he'd realized she was asking about his prior sexual history.

"I was so embarrassed by the jealously that implied." She angled a look his way. "I don't know if you ever realized how much I wanted to take back that question."

"But then you would have been deprived of my so very suave answer."

She laughed so hard she almost choked on a French fry. Two swallows of soda later, she wiped the corner of her mouth. "It was one for the history books."

At the same time, they said, "In a deer stand."

She started laughing again, and he couldn't help but join in. It felt good, just being together without all the subtexts and stress.

The two recliners were positioned side by side by the flickering firelight. Pots of blooming daffodils and violets beckoned. Hollie lay back on her recliner, dark brown hair splayed like a crown. Her eyes fluttered shut for a moment before blinking open, gazing upward.

Settling into his own recliner, Jacob sank into the plump cushions as he let his own gaze travel upward and settle on the Big Dipper. For a moment, they lay listening to the melody of crickets, swaying tree limbs, and the distant timbre of owls.

Jacob turned his head so he could see Hollie. "I'm glad we're getting to enjoy the garden together. We sure put enough hours into planning it."

She must have felt his stare because she turned, rolling onto her side. Chin and cheek cupped with one hand, dark wavy tendrils spilling over, she let out a sigh. "I thought for sure that Charlotte would turn in her resignation when we spelled out our vision in so, so very much detail."

"But she just dug in, went to work and made it even better. Even down to adding the butterfly house."

Her eyebrows pinched together as she searched his face. She bit her lip, a shadow chasing through her expression before she avoided his gaze.

Could she possibly be jealous? He'd certainly never given her cause to be, and the possibility that she might think as much now startled him.

Jacob shook his head. "Don't even think it."

"Think what?" she asked evasively.

"I know you too well. And to be clear, I'm not attracted to Charlotte." He swung his feet to the ground and sat on the edge of the lounger. "I'm only attracted to you."

She opened her mouth to speak, and he held up a hand to stop her. He needed to say this, to make it clear so there was no misunderstanding. There'd been far too much miscommunication between them.

"We were first lovers," he continued, taking her hands in his. "Our entire sexual history, all the preferences, wants and needs are tangled up in each other. Only each other."

She stared back at him silently, with wide blue eyes awash in emotion.

"Hollie, my dear, that has always been enough for me. That has been more than enough. Our chemistry is off the charts, and the thought of anyone else? My mind can't even go there."

Her lips parted. With surprise? But then her tongue swept lightly across her lips, an involuntary gesture he knew too well. Without question. Because, yes, he knew her body, had learned every signal.

Right now, Hollie wanted him every bit as much as he wanted her.

He lifted her hands to his mouth and grazed kisses across her knuckles. A soft purr of encouragement resonated in her throat, sliding free. And that was all the reassurance he needed.

Jacob angled forward to kiss his wife.

Chapter Ten

Her husband. Her lover.

She'd missed sex with him, the intimacy. They'd always connected on this level, at least. And after the gut-wrenching day they'd had with Lonnie's heart attack scare, she needed this.

She needed Jacob.

He reclined her on the lounger, kissing her in such a thorough and leisurely way, as if they had all the time in the world. As if their love wasn't drawing to a close.

But she didn't want to think about that now, or about Lonnie, or any other worries. She just wanted to feel, to savor the sweep of his tongue that carried a hint of saltiness from their shared dinner and a tang of bittersweet memories. He cupped her face, then caressed down her shoulder, along her arm in such a delicious glide, arousing in its pure simplicity.

She eased her head back and said, "Take me to our bedroom. Now, please."

Heat flared in his eyes as he stroked through her hair. "Are you sure this is what you want?"

"I'm in doubt of a lot of things. And I have no idea what's in store for tomorrow. But right now, for tonight, I don't question this for a moment." She drew in his scent, his oaky cologne, hands wandering up his arms. Feeling and treasuring the tensing of muscles beneath her fingertips.

A sigh shuddered through him. "I'm so glad. You have no idea how glad."

"I think I do." She looped her arms around his neck.

"Then why are we still talking when we could be in bed?" He slid an arm under her legs, another around her back, and scooped her up against his chest.

"Fantastic point." Because she feared if they carried on the conversation for much longer, some-how, they would stumble into one of those discussions that drove a wedge between them. Sex didn't solve everything. But right now, it was something.

Hollie sealed her mouth to his again, letting the blissful feeling sweep her away as his footsteps ate up the space leading into their bedroom, their blue velvet haven she'd created just for them. He shouldered the doors closed again, shutting out the world.

Slowly, he set her on her feet, and she relished every subtle rasp of his clothes against her as she slid downward, her arms still hooked around his neck. Which was a good thing since her knees weren't too steady. She'd denied herself this for too long. Her toes curled into the plush rug, every nerve in her body firing to life.

Urgency coursed through her veins. "We're wearing entirely too many clothes."

"Oh, trust me. I noticed," he said with a low chuckle. "I was trying to be a gentleman and go slow."

She pressed ever closer to him as she whispered softly, "What if I said that I don't want you to take your time? That I want you now. Right now. We can do leisurely afterward. And afterward again."

A sexy grin spread across his face. "Yes, ma'am. I do appreciate your vote of confidence, and I'll do my best to deliver."

His hands glided up to her shoulders as she reached for his belt buckle. With a synchronicity born of decades as lovers, they swept away each other's clothes, leaving a trail of cotton and lace on their way across the room.

In a tangle of arms and legs, they fell onto the mattress. How long had it been since they shared this bed? Too long.

He stretched over her with a rightness that took her breath away. The velvet comforter caressed her back, and she hooked a leg around Jacob. Then he slid inside her, taking his time with a restraint that drew out the sensation until her fingers twisted in the sheets. Until finally, finally, her husband was home.

And when he moved, her thoughts scattered. She lost herself in the sensation, in the rightness of being together with Jacob, her only lover. His hands stroked and lingered along all the places that teased her desire higher. The beauty of knowing each other so well. Her hands moved by memory to caress him, drawing soft moans from him, his pleasure increasing hers. His whispered words steamed through her.

All her senses went on heightened alert, taking in the world around her at a heightened level. The scent of flowers on the bedside table. The gentle rasp of his beard-stubbled cheek pressed to hers. The sound of a low fire crackling in the hearth, chasing away the chill of a mountain evening and throwing a warm glow across his body.

Months without him gathered the sensation tighter and tighter inside her…until she just let go, allowed the feelings to sweep her away. Her release powered through her, shattered her, then put her back together again. The intensity of her cries was matched by his as he found his completion, his handsome face taut in the firelight.

Locking her arms tighter around him, she gathered him closer, not ready to let go of this moment. She stroked along the back of his neck, letting the aftershocks ripple through her.

"Hollie…" he whispered against her neck.

Even now, the touch of his breath sent waves of awareness down her spine. If only she could bottle this moment, sip it slowly on the dark days, this time when there was nothing between them but pleasure. Hollie's arms still locking them here where she could feel the steady rise and fall of his chest against her.

"Shhh…" she whispered back. "Not now."

She didn't want anything to steal even a minute from this night, determined to push away concerns until the morning.

Jacob eased to his side, gathering her close as his breathing slowed, settling into the steady pattern of a light nap. Jacob's heartbeat cadence was a salve on her aching soul.

She was grateful he'd given her this—not just the time together, but holding each other afterward without a painful discussion. Without a reminder of what the future held.

His arm slid over her, his hand settling on her stomach, right over the pale scars. In an instant, the mood shifted, the pleasure evaporating. This pocket of time she'd tried desperately to use as a life-renewing experience was broken through gentle fingertips on her still-healing emotional wound. Enchantment always seemed to recede from them, even in this sacred place that had healed so many hurts.

And she couldn't escape the sense that in his sleep, barriers gone, he'd revealed himself. That he was still connected to her out of a sense of protectiveness and obligation.

She looked away, staring out the window as willows and elms swayed. Bright moonlight and cast dark, overbearing shadows into their bedroom tonight. Shadows tiptoed into the room, and shadows caressed her mind, her thoughts, as she ran a thumb over one of Jacob's hands.

In sleep, the brush of her fingertips caused him to hold tighter, nestle into the pool of her hair. Tears threatened and then formed in the corners of her eyes. Her vision became a blur, a mirror of the wreckage of last two decades with the man she still loved so much that the ache was physical.

Even with the out-of-this-world sex, the chemistry they shared, that wasn't enough to save them.

Freddy didn't want to go.

Except he couldn't run away again. He'd promised. And he wouldn't walk out on his brothers and sister.

So, he was stuck trying to pretend that he wasn't freaking out that they would be leaving tomorrow. He was supposed to pretend to enjoy the whole bird-watching outing this morning. They'd taken a hayride out to a clearing in the woods. Now they were sitting on blankets and having to be super still and quiet. Ugh.

Mr. Lonnie's son was supposed to lead it, but there'd been some kind of change in plans that no one was telling the kids about.

No surprise there. He was getting used to his life changing all the time, thanks to the grown-ups, with no warning and no explanations.

The extra "babysitter" following him around

hadn't been half bad, once he'd gotten used to the fact they didn't trust him. Well, not that they should have after what he'd done. But he was glad he'd stuck around because, if he'd gone, he would have missed out on a lot of fun this week.

Other than today's bird-watching, sitting in the middle of a bunch of trees, getting bitten by mosquitoes. One of those pesky bloodsuckers buzzed right by his ear. He did his best to swat it, but the mosquito was fast.

They'd given him a booklet with pictures of different kinds of birds. He was supposed to check off how many he saw. They would get prizes at the end, depending on how many they found.

The kids who couldn't read, like Elliot and Phillip, had a helper. But kids like him and Ivy were on the honor system. He wanted to know how they could prove he really saw it. He could just make up a bunch of stuff and they wouldn't know.

He remembered Mrs. O'Brien reminding him that he shouldn't tell lies. But it was hard. He didn't like his life. The one he made up was better.

Well, and it was fun to see the looks on people's faces when he came up with a really, really surprising story. Like when he told that librarian lady—Miss Susanna, the one who read them stories with a dog—that his dad got sick in the pan-

demic and his mama was overseas in the military.
She'd said that was very sad, but something in her
eyes told him she didn't believe him.

Then she'd nicely told him to go back to his
seat on the quilt so she could finish reading them
the story about the birds and flowers they would
see today. The book had actually been kinda interesting.

He lifted his pencil to check off five birds on
the list…and then a flutter up in the tree caught
his attention. It sang back down at him. He looked
at the list again, then studied the pictures. There
were songbirds like sparrows and warblers. He
squinted back up at the tree, trying to determine
if the yellow feathers he saw were a warbler or not.

Then there were the pretty birds, like a blue-
bird or a red-tailed hawk. Freddy wanted to see a
red-tailed hawk real bad. His last schoolteacher
had read a story about a knight that protected his
family from goblins and had a pet hawk. Since
his parents were gone, Freddy figured he was like
that knight, too.

The bottom of the page had a bunch more bird
types. He was pretty sure the screech owl was
out mostly at night, so if he marked that one, they
might know he wasn't being honest.

And he was trying really hard to be better even

though he wanted to stomp around and pitch a fit over leaving tomorrow. Freddy looked up from his sheet of paper and saw Mr. O'Brien approaching. He had a white cowboy hat on, and he was smiling as his boots crunched over the twigs.

Freddy let the paper rest in his lap. He was sitting crisscross and stuck the pencil between his legs. "Where've you been? I was kinda thinking I would see you around when we were looking at constel...constella...looking at the stars."

"Constellations." Jacob took a seat next to him on a nearby tree root. "I had a friend who was sick, so I went to the hospital to see him. You may remember him—Mr. Lonnie."

Freddy's eyes widened. The last thing he wanted was for someone else to not be okay. He remembered how his parents had been taken to a hospital. That seemed to be a bad place to wind up. "Santa Claus? Is he okay?"

"He's going to be fine. Thank you for asking."

"What's wrong with him?" Freddy took his baseball hat off and played with the rim of the hat. He had been afraid to ask, but he needed to know what happened to Mr. Lonnie.

"He had a small heart attack." Mr. O'Brien's eyes looked worried. "The doctors think that medicine, more walking, and some changes in what he eats will take care of it."

Freddy resisted the urge to say his mom had died of a heart attack. Putting his baseball cap on backwards, he looked up at Mr. Jacob. "If I draw him a card, will you be sure he gets it?"

"That's a really good idea. I'm sure he would like that," he said like he meant it, not in that way that sometimes adults spoke when they were just trying to make the kids feel better.

"No problem." Back when his kindergarten teacher broke her leg, his mom had him make a card. She'd helped him with the words and the scissors.

Maybe he could glue a bird feather to the card. He could tell Ivy, Phillip and Elliot that story about the card to help them remember their mom. It made him sad that they didn't have as many memories of her as he did, and this was a good one to share. Plus, they could help him. It would sorta be like their mom was there in spirit.

A noise buzzed past his ear, something bigger than a mosquito.

Mr. O'Brien watched it, then pointed to a tall pine tree. "Look there, about halfway up. That's my favorite bird. Can you guess what it is?"

Freddy squinted up at the pine tree, shielding

his eyes from the sun so he could see better. This little bird moved really fast downward, closer until he could see it had a red throat. Freddy looked at the booklet, flipping through each page, glancing back and forth until… "Is it a hummingbird?"

"You're right. Way to go, kiddo." Mr. O'Brien gave him a high-five. "Have you had a good time this week?"

"Yeah." He tapped the pencil against his cheek.

"What was your favorite thing to do?" When Freddy shrugged, Jacob continued, "It helps me to know what people enjoy the most. Then I can make extra sure it's always on the schedule."

"I liked riding the horses. But there aren't horses at the group home." He looked up quickly, then down again. "But I probably won't be there long."

"Why is that?"

Freddy saw the skeptical look on the guy's face and realized Mr. O'Brien was expecting him to tell a lie about his parents. And suddenly he didn't want that look to stay on his face. "They're looking for a foster home for me to go to."

"How do you feel about that?"

"I dunno." Afraid. He rubbed the pencil between his hands, not looking at Mr. O'Brien at all. "Some of the other kids have scary stories."

"Do you believe them?"

Yes, he did. And it made his stomach hurt. Not just for himself, but for his brothers and sister, too. "I've never met a foster parent before, so I don't know."

Mr. O'Brien took off his Stetson. "Hollie and I were foster parents for a while."

He bet they were good ones. But they weren't fostering children anymore. Probably got tired of kids like him causing trouble and eating up all their snacks. It stung to think that Mr. O'Brien was a fake, pretending like he cared what birds Freddy saw.

"Well, uh, that's cool." Freddy opened up his bird booklet again. "I gotta finish this so I can win some prizes. Can we stop talking? You're making a lot of noise, and I don't want you to scare off the birds."

Freddy kept his eyes down, waiting. Finally, Mr. O'Brien pushed to his feet. "Sure thing, champ. See you later."

A lump swelled in Freddy's throat. He felt really alone, which was crazy since there were so many people around. But he knew what it was like to have people care, have a family that loved each other. And what he had now wasn't even close.

Freddy picked up the pencil again, opened his bird book, and checked off every single one on the list.

* * *

Hollie had never found it so difficult to focus on work.

But then, the sex with her husband had been off the charts. They'd made up for lost time through the night. She'd worked out months' worth of tension, which had left her exhausted.

In the best of ways. And the most confusing.

Lord, she was a mess, and the timing couldn't have been much worse. The latest family event for Allegra was tense, to say the least, with the mother of the groom and the mother of the bride lobbing thinly veiled insults at each other. Hopefully, they could keep them busy enough to make it through the next hour's activity in the lodge's gathering room.

She went through the motions of assisting guests and making polite conversation, all on autopilot as her mind swirled with thoughts of Jacob. Before, during all their platonic dates, she'd been curious about what game he was playing—she'd wanted answers but somehow never got around to confronting him. Had she been afraid of the answer? Was that why, when they finally got around to sex, she didn't want to talk anymore?

So much had happened, and she finally had the space to think it through for some kind of understanding. Lonnie's heart attack scare had certainly driven her to Jacob's bed, but also made her realize how fragile her connection was to Jacob now. His platonic dates had also made her realize how fast she was losing the ability to read him, and she couldn't deny that it scared her. So much so, she'd leaped at the opportunity for the night with him as a way to reconnect, if only briefly.

So, what now?

Ashlynn was leading the guests in a sensory activity—using dried flower petals to make sachets and soy candles to be given as party favors for the reception. They'd coordinated the flower colors and ribbons to match the bride's palette for the wedding—pale pink and tan.

Sighs of appreciation swelled through the craft space set up in one of the lodge's meeting rooms. A fireplace crackled with electric flames to cast ambiance while being able to control the temperature. Allegra was surrounded by her bridesmaids, lifting different mixes of dried petals to sniff.

"If any of you get a case of the jitters—over getting married or just because of standing up in front of everyone—try an exercise in grounding. Breathe in deeply, then exhale. Catalog all the scents. And at a big wedding like this one, there will be plenty." Hollie dipped her candle just as she had done countless times before and offered a smile and wink to Allegra.

The grandmother of the groom lifted her sparkling champagne, raspberries floating. "Yes, such as how the chia cake will smell like hay."

Uh-oh.

A twitter of laughter rippled through the attendees from the groom's family. A satisfied, subtle smirk creased the woman's face as the sconces in the room glinted off her oversized silver hoop earrings.

Allegra straightened in her chair, her bridesmaids clustering around her protectively. The bride's eyes were wide, tears gathering in the corners.

The mother of the bride, however, was not as constrained. She shot to her feet, her blond bob swinging with aggressive energy. "I have had enough of the way you talk to my daughter. This should be the most special time of her life, and now she's under all this pressure—"

"Pressure from you," Allegra's future grandmother-in-law retorted as she rose to her feet, her patterned maxi skirt stirring with the motion.

Although at this rate, the woman might not achieve the in-law status.

Hollie stepped forward, searching for a way to

smooth the ruffled feathers, a struggle given how fried she was emotionally. Too bad she couldn't just dump a bucket of flower petals over both women and call it a day.

"Ladies, can I interest you in an afternoon at our spa?" As soon as the words fell out of her mouth, she remembered that Patsy and Lonnie were out of commission. What a time to realize how much she depended on them. She scrambled for an alternative. "I can comp you two hours at our hot springs in the cave. The water there is so relaxing and restorative—"

The mother of the bride adjusted her white cardigan that was dotted with clusters of red-and-pink flowers. She looked down her nose and scoffed. "The last thing I want is to spend more time with her."

The grandmother of the groom narrowed her eyes, her voice dipping dangerously. "Well, then it's a lucky thing we'll make sure we never cross paths at holidays."

Standing, Allegra reached out a hand. "Please, the last thing I want is a rift. Family is important to Simon."

Simon's grandmother said, "Then it's a shame this is what the rest of your life together will look like."

Allegra's mother closed in, face red. And the volley of words went back and forth, insults and anger escalating until the bride was in tears.

Hollie looked to Ashlynn for ideas or support, but her assistant was on the floor, scooping up the pile of petals that had been knocked to the floor in the fray. Someone needed to do something fast. This was escalating at a dangerously intense rate when emotions were already running high.

She clapped her hands together in a manner she hoped was just loud enough to gain everyone's attention without seeming like she was playing referee.

Even though that's exactly what she was doing.

"Rather than the hot springs, how about let's go outside for party drinks and hors d'oeuvres." She would scramble with Ashlynn to set up stations that encouraged guests to stay very far apart from each other. "Our chef makes the most delicious corn relish dip. It's famous throughout the state."

She motioned to Ashlynn, who, in that wonderful way of hers, managed to read the unspoken direction. Ashlynn made fast tracks toward the kitchen, while Hollie threw open the French doors leading out to a massive patio, praying the guests would take the hint.

And thank goodness, as if those open doors

uncorked a bottle, the heated guests poured out into the covered rustic dining area. So perfect she wondered why she hadn't thought of it in the first place.

Just being outdoors swept away some of the tension with each gust of cool mountain air. The music of birds lilted along the breeze. It was idyllic. It was home.

A cry split through her musing. She pivoted fast and found…

Allegra was running toward her fiancé as he strode out of the forest from a morning of bird-watching. She stopped in front of him, sobbing.

"Simon, I just can't do this anymore. It's too stressful. I don't want to come between you and your family." She clutched the straps of his binoculars. "I love you with all my heart, but I have to call off the wedding."

Chapter Eleven

Pandemonium exploded all around Jacob.

Allegra was sobbing. Her friends and her mother were glaring daggers at Simon and his family. His grandmother was on her phone speaking far too loudly about how lucky Simon was to escape this family.

Milo's camera was clicking like a woodpecker at work after two pots of coffee.

This was the last way Jacob wanted to spend the day. He'd been chewing over Freddy's situation the whole way home from the bird-watching trip, regretting he'd somehow alienated the kid he'd tried hard to connect with. Then, his head was still spinning from the surprise turn of events with Hollie from the night before. He finally had his wife back in his bed, just when he'd feared he'd lost her for good. Now, he had to figure out a way to keep her there.

Tough to do when he hadn't understood why she'd finally reached out for him after all this time. Had anything changed for her? Nothing was more important to him than repairing his broken marriage. Yet the world was in chaos, and it was up to him and Hollie to repair things.

Hollie stepped up beside him, hugging her arms around herself as she pitched her voice low for his ears only. "There's so much that's gone right about the other weddings. Even Lonnie and Patsy's ceremony turned out alright in the end since he's going to be released tomorrow."

Jacob looked at the churning emotions before him. Simon's grandmother stood, hands on her hips in what appeared to be a staring match with Allegra's mother. The two matriarchs seethed from across the room. Simon sat on one of the red cushioned wooden chairs, blanched face between his hands.

Still, Jacob figured he had a better shot of fixing this mess than his own screwed-up life. Because at least for this knotty problem, he'd have his wife's help.

Jacob let out a low whistle. "And now all people will remember is this whole left-at-the-altar moment."

Hollie massaged her temples. "We should have been prepared for something like this to happen with at least one couple."

Shifting, Jacob angled closer, his arm brushing hers as he leaned in to whisper, "But why did it have to be the couple slated for the largest ceremony on the very last day?"

Hollie's bright eyes shone with determination as she looked up at him. "I'm not giving up just yet. Maybe we can salvage something from this debacle—for our sake and for theirs." Hollie touched his arm lightly. "Keep them from killing each other for thirty seconds. I'll be right back."

His wife bustled away with an enticing twitch of her hips, disappearing into the lodge for a lot less than thirty seconds. She charged back out the door with a portable microphone in her hand.

"Excuse me, everyone. Excuse me." She raised her voice. "Hey, can I have your attention please?"

The rumble of grousing eased, then quieted as Allegra and Simon's families turned toward Hollie. Tension simmered, mouths pressed tight as if holding back a flood of anger.

His wife offered a calm, professional smile, even though she unconsciously squeezed her hands so tightly together her knuckles turned bloodlessly white. "Clearly, emotions are running high. So we would like to make it easier for everybody to take a breath. We will be sending catered meals to each of your cabins. Ashlynn will take care of your orders."

Jacob could see Ashlynn moving into action, dividing the task in half so that one of the support staffers from the front desk spoke with Simon's clan, while Ashlynn approached Allegra's mother.

Then, Hollie pivoted toward the feuding couple sitting on opposite ends of pine patio table. "Simon and Allegra, come with me and my husband. We can chat in the garden about how you want to handle the next few days."

And not a single soul argued.

Smart of them.

Well, she'd sure handled that like the Hollie he knew so well. He'd missed seeing her feisty side.

Was it wrong of him that he wished she'd barrel into their private suite tonight and lay down the law about how they'd fix their relationship?

He could use that kind of clear, straightforward guidance.

Now, Hollie gestured with an invitation for the couple to rise from the table. Allegra's bottom lip wobbled as she filed behind Simon, whose jaw flexed with tension. Hollie led the way as they left the crowd behind, walking the perimeter of the lodge to the back entrance. She unlatched the wooden gate, which opened with a gentle push and a loud creak.

Jacob watched Simon's instinctive move to reach for Allegra's hand as she walked over the threshold and onto the canyon stone patio pavers. A small gesture that could almost go unnoticed, but Jacob had become acutely aware of these gestures, having experienced them himself this past year and a half.

But Simon held back, following Hollie and Allegra into the recesses of the garden patio. Hollie stopped beneath the pink flowering tree near the small wooden butterfly house Jacob had the landscaper add for Hollie's birthday.

Curious where his wife planned to go with this meeting, he let her take the lead. So he turned on the flame in the small firepit and set up four chairs.

"Let's talk. Just talk." Hollie motioned for the two to sit down in the high-back patio chairs with extra stuffed cushioning. They warily sat down, eyeing each other as they leaned back in their seats.

Jacob pulled his thoughts away from the recent make-out session he and Hollie had recently indulged in in this very space.

"Now that we're comfortable, maybe we could take stock of where we are before we try to figure out what's next," Hollie suggested lightly, counseling the couple as smoothly as any pro. "I think we all need to take a breath."

Jacob's thoughts ran back to Lonnie's suggestion for them, wondering if he needed to think about that more. There'd been half-hearted discussions about it in the past, and then they tabled it while they lost themselves in more work.

"Well, it's like this..." Allegra's voice was stilted. It took her three tries before she formed words without a sob escaping. Steadying herself by gripping the arms of the chair, she spoke, her vocal cords raw from crying. "Our families have never gotten along. If it's this bad now, how much worse will it be once we're married?"

Simon shifted in his chair, pain cutting lines into the corners of his mouth. "We could just move away. Very far away. I've always wanted to climb Mount Kilimanjaro."

Allegra dropped her grip on the chair and turned to Hollie with a huff of frustration. "See? This kind of flippant answer doesn't solve anything. They will still be a part of our lives, of every important occasion—even more so when we have kids. I just can't take all the digs about our back-to-nature style of living. What are they going to say when they hear we want to live off the grid in a tiny house?"

"I'm not trying to avoid," Simon said gently. "I just want to keep things from escalating before the wedding. You've seen my grandma. I love her, but she's a pistol."

Fresh tears welled in Allegra's eyes. Messy strands of her brown hair were plastered to the tear tracks on her tan cheeks. "But what about after the wedding? What about the rest of our lives together? I can't live this way, waiting for the next bomb to drop every time our families are in the same space."

Jacob rested a hand on his chair's arm, stealing a glance at Hollie, who was nodding supportively at the conversation unfolding. He knew well that avoidance grew canyons in a relationship.

Jacob cleared his throat and leaned forward. "What do you think about setting some parameters for your families?"

Simon frowned. "Like how?"

Hollie edged closer to the fire pit, the spring mountain air chillier than normal. "The buzzword these days is *boundaries*. Spell out lovingly but very precisely what you expect in family gatherings at your home."

Allegra's eyes widened in horror as she lifted a dismissive hand. "But that means when they start a fight, we have to tell them to leave. I don't think I can do that."

For a moment, birdsong and crackling fire echoed in the small patio. Hollie looked over at him, her blue eyes full of wisdom and experience. Jacob met her gaze, that unspoken language passing through them.

Finally, Jacob cut the silence. "You don't have to micromanage every bit of the gathering."

And just like that, his wife picked up the thread of his thought and started weaving. "Simply focus on the basics, whatever the two of you decide those are. Can you do that?"

Simon scrubbed the back of his neck. "I think we have to. Otherwise this won't get better. And I don't want to lose you."

Allegra pushed the strands of her tear-dampened hair off her face and tucked them behind her ears.

A wobbly smile creased her face. "I don't want to lose you either. Maybe we should just elope."

Simon shook his head. "Or maybe we could start now in setting those boundaries. We remind our families this is our wedding. We tell them we want them to celebrate with us. But only if they're willing to actually celebrate. No fighting. No lobbing criticisms."

"Awww," Allegra's voice hitched. "You would do that for me?"

"Of course, sweetie. We can tell them first thing tomorrow." Simon gripped her hands, staring into her eyes for a moment, before turning to Jacob and Hollie. "Thank you for your help. If our families ask where we are, we're going camping."

Jacob watched the two of them walk away, each with an arm around the other. Would they last? He knew their road ahead wouldn't be as simple as a conversation made it sound. Following through on boundaries wouldn't be easy. But it was a path out of the forest they were in, and he really hoped it would work for them.

No one should go through the pain of what they'd been through, or the grief of a split. As much as he'd made inroads with Hollie, he'd learned over the years that there were no guarantees. All the more reason to make the most of the moment together.

He extended a hand to Hollie, an invitation. For a moment he thought she would claim a work obligation. But then she reached for him, clasping her fingers around his to walk toward the doors leading to the suite they'd once shared. The gift of what she offered humbled him. Made him hope they could still figure this out. He opened the door and swept her into his arms.

Together—for now.

The next morning, Hollie needed to keep herself busy, which was a lucky thing since getting the kids ready to return to the group home would have been hectic on any day. But doing so on so little sleep was beyond challenging.

Hollie sorted through gift bags, double-checking to make sure they were labeled appropriately for each child. Her hands shook as she got to the four bags labeled for the Hudson kids.

Clouds blanketed the morning sky even though the weather forecast hadn't called for rain. In the distance, thunder rumbled. Every time a thunder crack sounded, the Hudson kids clapped excitedly, whooping in some kind of game. Hollie glanced at the darkening clouds, hoping the weather would hold off just a while longer while the children loaded into the vehicle.

There were two vans with the group home's logo on the side and one minivan, also with a logo on the side, but this vehicle had been driven by the extra employee who'd come later to keep an eye on Freddy.

At least the big blowup between Allegra's and Simon's families had settled down, thanks to some mediation from Allegra's benevolent uncle Samuel. Albeit things were still tense. But apparently seeing how their behavior had almost wrecked the couple's future had made an impression.

Some of their relatives had decided to stay for the wedding. A few others had opted to leave— which made an already busy morning even more hectic. Once they'd returned from the camping trip, Simon had held his ground in not caving to pacify. He'd made it clear they welcomed all, but that no sniping or backbiting was allowed.

How was she going to handle this kind of mayhem on her own? She and Jacob had always been a team, and that teamwork served them well. It was the key to the Top Dog Dude Ranch success. Would dividing their efforts lead to the collapse of everything they'd built? Would they have nothing left, not even the solace of work?

For now she just had to get the kids on the bus without mishap and without crying. Because she had to admit, saying goodbye to these little ones was tougher than she'd expected. Tears had blurred her eyes off and on all morning, so much so, she worked overtime at keeping herself away from Milo's too-perceptive lens.

Jacob lifted his black Stetson from his head, facing the Hudson kids. "Thank you for spending the week with us."

Phillip peered at Hollie with seriousness beyond his years, his normal rowdiness subdued. He placed a freckled hand on his chest, and lifted his chin. "I wish we didn't have to go. This place is fun."

"I'm glad to hear that. We sure try hard to come up with activities that kids will enjoy, too."

Ivy looked up, her eyes wide behind her glasses. "You mean 'pack-tivities,' don't you?"

Elliot had angled his body slightly away from the group, stealing glances at his siblings every few moments. His attention was mostly focused beyond the pickup area to the red barn and adjoining paddocks. A faint smile crossed his shadowed face as Nutmeg was turned out in the pasture.

Jacob chuckled. "You're absolutely right. What was your favorite pack-tivity?"

Phillip rocked back on his heels. "I liked camping in a tent in the barn."

Freddy swept off his ball cap and bent the brim. "I thought the bird-watching was actually kinda cool."

Ivy nudged her glasses further up the bridge of her nose. "I enjoyed floating down the stream on the inner tube."

Hollie wished she could have brought Scottie with her to say goodbye to the kids, but with Lonnie and Patsy away, they were shorthanded. "And what about you, Elliot? What pack-tivity will you remember most?"

Elliot dropped his llama puppet and silently stared off into the distance. Freddy picked up the puppet and dusted it off. He held out his hand to give it back, but his younger brother ignored him, shuffling a few steps closer to the line to leave.

Freddy's face fell, too much sadness in it for one so young. He folded the felt llama flat and tucked the puppet into his back pocket. "I guess we should get going."

The children from the group home lined up single file. The line inched forward as the children disappeared into the first van, but Elliot's brows furrowed in distress. Freddy took him by the hand. Elliot tugged, digging his heels into the ground, his tennis shoes sinking into the mud. He shook his head, not budging.

"Come on, Elliot," Freddy said. "We have to go."

Elliot pulled harder and harder, his eyes locked on the silver minivan.

Sighing, Freddy put his ball cap back on. "Buddy, we're going in the bigger van."

Ivy stepped up. "Yeah, the wheels on the bus go round and round. Remember when Mom used to sing that on trips? Come on. It's okay."

Elliot didn't even look at them, intensity building in his little body, his gaze locked. "I hear you."

The words were precise. Clear.

Hollie jolted. Could he possibly be recovering from whatever had made him retreat into his *Dr. Dolittle* world? Could he be ready to communicate with people?

His twin and his sister stepped up expectantly. Then Elliot yanked his hand away, rushing to the minivan.

"I hear you, I hear you, I hear you," he chanted.

Elliot threw himself on the ground, diving under the minivan. Hollie's stomach lurched, and she looked around frantically for Shawna.

Jacob rushed forward and grabbed his feet encased in muddy tennis shoes. "Come on, buddy. It's time to go now—"

He'd only succeeded in partially removing the child from under the bus when, frowning, Jacob rocked back on his heels. He tipped his ear toward the hood of the vehicle, then tucked up underneath as well in the dirt right where Elliot had been a moment ago.

The speed with which her husband moved warmed her heart and reminded her of her concerns about their success being tied into their teamwork. Was she actually having second thoughts about moving?

Or was she just making excuses to stay here with him because she was too scared to walk away?

Blinking through her confusion, she forced herself to focus on the crisis at hand. The four Hudson children were gathered around the minivan near Jacob's jeans-clad legs sticking out.

"Well what do you know? Elliot, you clever boy. I hear it, too." Jacob slid back out and sat up, his back covered in mud. "There's a stubborn little kitten stuck up in the engine, and until it comes out, there's no way this vehicle can leave."

A woman's voice filtered through the crowd. "I think the Top Dog magic had turned into a Top Dog curse."

A man's voice chased right after it on the wind.

"Can you believe all the things going wrong? Before long, I bet we're gonna be swarmed with bullfrogs."

Stuck underneath the minivan, Jacob was trying to pinpoint the exact location of the tricky kitty. The rippling negative comments of the guests congregating drifted on the breeze.

How many motors was he going to have to take apart during what should have been two weeks of wedding parties? First the refrigerator and now the engine of a county group home minivan. Bad luck on top of bad luck.

One thing was for sure. No matter how many treats they offered or how many toys they dangled to entice the animal, the kitten wasn't coming out on its own. Which meant they had to continue taking apart the motor until they could reach the stubborn little critter.

Rain clouds turned darker and heavier. Thunder rolled again, louder.

And Milo was taking far too many photos of each and every mishap.

At least Jacob had help. Although he could see the headline now. *Come to the Top Dog Dude Ranch, where we'll put you to work.*

Samuel Woodley—Allegra's uncle—was apparently an incredible mechanic as well as a business mogul. He and Thomas—who'd helped with the broken freezer—had joined forces to save the kitten while Hollie kept the kids from going stir-crazy while waiting to leave. They were currently under the hood while Jacob stayed under the van.

"Thomas," Samuel's voice drifted down, "could you pass me the other socket wrench? Thanks."

Hollie knelt beside the van, her face coming into view as she whispered, "How much longer do you think this is going to take?"

He wished he knew. As much as Jacob had tried to make time for romancing her into staying put here, it seemed that everything conspired against them finding time alone together for anything more than sex. Not that he was complaining about the time in the bedroom. He just wanted... more...more time with Hollie. More of a chance to reclaim what they'd had in the early days.

"Well," Jacob said, holding a flashlight and staring up into the engine, looking past the belts toward the direction of the kitten's mewling, "if the kitty jumps out—which could happen at any moment—that would sure help things."

Shawna eased into view behind her. "Is there something I can do to help? Should I turn on the motor to startle the cat away?"

"No!" Jacob, Samuel and Thomas shouted at the same time.

Milo's camera clicked. *Snap. Snap.*

Jacob just barely missed bumping his head as he reached out, waving for their attention. "We need to be careful not to, uh, harm the cat."

"Oh. Right," Shawna gasped in a horrified voice. "That could be pretty traumatic."

That was putting it mildly. He shuddered to think of how badly that could go—or what photos Milo would capture.

"Hopefully the kitten will jump free on his or her own sooner rather than later," Jacob said, easing out enough to see Hollie and Shawna better. "But even if that happens, we would still have to put all the parts back together that we've removed so far. I'm guessing that would take at least an hour."

Shawna's eyebrows pinched together. "And if the cat stays up in there?"

Samuel wiped his hands on a rag. "We could be looking at hours."

Thomas tapped a wrench against his hand. "And that's provided the rain holds off."

Another clap of thunder split the air.

Shawna pursed her lips together, sighed, then said, "Alright, that helps to know. Thank you for giving it to me straight. I'm going to send the other two vans back now. I can stay with this vehicle until it's safe to go."

Jacob pushed to his feet, swiping the back of his wrist over his sweaty forehead. "That makes sense."

Snap. Snap.

"I have one request." Shawna rested her clipboard on her hip.

"Whatever we can do to help."

"I'm concerned about sending Freddy back with all the others. With bathroom breaks and dinner breaks, what if he slips away again?"

Hollie rubbed a hand over her mouth as she did when thinking things through. "The vans do look packed to the gills with all of their extra Top Dog gear we gave them, thanks to Mr. Woodley. What if Freddy and his siblings stay? Just so Freddy won't get too stressed without them. They seem very attached to one another."

Now, that stunned Jacob silent. He'd thought Hollie was keeping her distance from the children. He certainly hadn't wanted to do anything that would bring another ounce of pain to her eyes. But then, she'd always had such a big heart.

And he didn't have any more clue now than before how to protect his wife from additional heartbreak. His whole marriage lately felt like every bit as much of an exercise in futility as trying to lure the kitten out of the engine block. No matter how hard he tried, he was going at it from the wrong approach, and he was running out of options fast.

With Hollie and the kitten.

Shawna glanced back and forth from the Hudson kids to Hollie, then over to Jacob. "Are you sure you don't mind? I'll personally keep watch over all four of them."

Hollie touched her arm lightly. "It's absolutely no trouble at all. Now, what can I do to help you get the other children on their way?"

No sooner had the words left her mouth than the clouds opened up, releasing a deluge of rain.

Snap. Snap.

Chapter Twelve

Rain hammered harder than Hollie's heart in her stressed-out chest.

Soaking wet, she shoved her sleeves up and stood behind the counter at the ranch's ice-cream shop. The four Hudson kids were in a line in front of the glass counter, tasting different flavors in a tiny sample cups with paw print flourishes.

The local meteorologist had really let them all down today. But she had to admit, she was glad for the moment away from Jacob. Not to sift through her feelings, but rather to stop thinking about them so much for a little while, just to catch her breath.

Once the massive storm clouds had unleashed

their fury on the Top Dog Dude Ranch, Jacob had thrown a tarp over the engine parts and declared that operation on hold until the weather cleared. Hollie had sent Shawna and the Hudsons to the ice-cream parlor, which gave her access to her small office off of the shop's kitchen.

It hadn't been easy, but she'd adjusted the location for the day's outdoor events, losing herself in the activity, welcoming the way it helped her push away unwelcome emotions. In particular, she'd changed Constance's bridal shower from a brunch under a sprawling oak to princess makeovers in the spa.

The wedding was supposed to take place tomorrow by the waterfall, but it was already flooding. Ashlynn and Charlotte were hard at work decorating the lodge's social hall into a fairy-tale castle full of flowers. Thank goodness that the couple expecting a baby had already said their vows the day before by the hot springs—a fitting locale since they were Top Dog employees—then headed into town to the hospital for her scheduled induction. Briggs and Eleanor were now the proud parents of a healthy baby girl.

Hollie swept a hank of wet hair off her brow.

Scents of cinnamon and vanilla clung to the space filled with wrought-iron tables and chairs on the patio as well as inside. There were two areas for dining in the shop, one with human treats and one with pooch treats. Ice cream. Cakes. Cookies.

The dogs around here got treats too—pup-sicles and pup-cakes. Ziggy, Bandit and Scottie sat on the dog beds, eating a pup-cake shaped like a paw and a tiny paper cup filled with frozen yogurt.

Ivy arched up on her toes, pressing her nose to the glass as she squinted behind her glasses. "I want the cookies and cream, with chocolate syrup on top, please."

Phillip jumped like he was on a pogo stick. "Cotton candy flavor with sprinkles. Please. And thank you."

Elliot pointed to the strawberry and to the gummy bear toppings.

Rain tapped on the roof while Freddy chewed his bottom lip, thinking. Then he blurted, "Would it be okay if I had two scoops of the birthday cake ice cream with lots of whipped cream?"

Hollie nodded. "Coming right up."

Once the siblings were settled at a table, Hollie strode over to Shawna and passed her a waffle cone full of vanilla ice cream. Hollie sat at the table with her own cone of praline pecan. "Shawna, is it my imagination, or was it a big deal that Elliot pointed to ask for his ice cream?

Even though he wasn't speaking, he also wasn't using a conversation with animals to communicate indirectly."

Shawna's eyebrows lifted. "That's very insightful of you to notice, especially for someone who's not a social worker. I know I've said it before, but you're really good with the kids."

Hearing that jabbed at old wounds. She knew she was good with children. She enjoyed them. But she also couldn't keep saying goodbye, whether through miscarriages or failed adoption.

"I love my career here, but I want—wanted— to be a mother. When I was little, each day before school, I would make sure each of my dolls was dressed and tucked in."

"That's sweet." Shawna reached across the ice-cream table to pat her hand. "I'm sorry you've had such a rough journey to fulfilling that dream."

"I saved those dolls to share with my children one day." Hollie's shoulders sloped down as she concentrated on her ice-cream cone.

Shawna gave Hollie's hand a slight squeeze. "That could still happen."

The simple statement made her stomach twist as every cell inside her shouted no. Would she even want that dream without Jacob?

Her marriage was over, her fertility in the tank,

and adoption had shredded what was left of her heart. And there was nothing anyone could say to make it better. Friends had tried so many words of comfort. Counselors had offered her wise advice— even if Jacob wouldn't attend.

And yet, her life was still a mess.

She thought she'd let go of those dreams, but she'd been fooling herself, hugging vestiges tight like a child clutching her dolls.

It was time to truly let go, once and for all.

She scooted back her chair. "Ivy, when you're done with your ice cream, I have some dolls you can play with. They even have books that go with each one. If you like them, you're welcome to take them with you when you go."

Ivy nodded her head, fast, eager, the rubber band on her thick ponytail sliding perilously low. "Yes, please, yes—"

Her squeals were cut short by the door swinging open, bells chiming. Wind gusted in, sweeping in sheeting rain along with it.

Jacob strode inside looking too handsome, even drenched, droplets sliding off the brim of his Stetson. He unzipped his rain jacket and pulled out a little orange fluff ball. "Who wants to pet the kitten?"

Why did letting go have to be so very hard?

* * *

Jacob had decided the rain was his friend.

Even though they were up to their eyeballs in work accommodating the changes brought on by the never-ending storm, Hollie couldn't avoid him. They'd made it through Thomas and Constance's fairy-tale wedding, and the reception was in full swing.

Thomas twirled Constance, the older woman's puffy wedding dress fluttering as she tossed her head back in delight. The guests, like Constance, all were adorned with tiaras and jewels—part of the bride's vision for a happily-ever-after reception. Constance had arranged for a display of costume jewelry to be available to all her guests.

And the women absolutely glittered as they danced beneath arches full of flowers. From the stage, a violinist and pianist supplied romantic tunes. Even the tapping of the rain on the roof seemed to go with the classical tunes.

The roads had washed out temporarily from all the rain. People who were going to check out were stuck, which caused a glut with last-minute arrivals of wedding guests who arrived just prior to this tsunami-like downpour. So they were making shuffles in cabin accommodations. Shawna and the Hudson children were going to stay in the suite Jacob had been occupying, and he was back to sharing a bed with Hollie.

Yep, he was digging this rain.

His boot tapped in time with the waltz, raindrops adding nature's percussion. Jacob's gaze found Hollie across the room, her elegant curves accentuated by the peach floor-length Grecian gown. Straps of lace flowers rested gently on her shoulders, and the smile on her face seemed brighter than the delicate tiara tucked into her upswept hair. Loose tendrils caressed her cheeks. She looked like a fantasy, and he wanted to join her.

Jacob strode across the dance floor and extended a hand. Waiting. Hoping for once something could be easy for them, if only for a simple dance.

Smiling, she stepped into his arms, and he wanted to tell himself it wasn't just for show. They seemed to have found a comfortable pattern these past few days. Soon, he would need to ask her outright if she would consider staying.

Was he delaying, trying to stretch out that fantasy moment?

Possibly. Was it wrong to hope that she would come to the conclusion on her own?

Her feet in satin slippers picked up the rhythm, step for step in synch with him. "Everything looks so lovely." She sighed. "I feel like I can say that since the project was Ashlynn and Charlotte's baby."

"Don't sell yourself short," Jacob whispered, his cheek resting against her head, the lilac scent of her teasing every breath. "You had plenty of input while juggling other weddings."

She waved away his compliment in the typical Hollie humble style. "Kendric and Natalie's Western wedding was a simple change."

Since the rain hadn't let up, rather than hold the ceremony and reception outdoors, they'd improvised the same decor in the barn—all doors open as they'd done with other events in the past.

"Not that simple, really." He banded his arm tighter around her waist, the tulle of her peach gown swirling around his legs in phantom caresses. "You just make it look easy."

"I'll admit that some of the other weddings were more of a challenge..." As she glided under the twinkling lights, the crystals along the beaded top of her gown glistened. "Like the Grecian garden theme and the Kentucky Derby vibe. But we pulled it off, even with the completely uncooperative weather, because we worked together."

The Hudson kids danced together, excitement radiating with every dance move they made, full of large flourishes and laughter. So very adorable.

They had been fun last-minute additions to the wedding party, and they were certainly enjoying the limelight at the reception. They were all decked out in clothes from the Top Dog gift shop. Ivy's flowy dress sported a wide bow, her hair in bouncy curls with a sparkling tiara. The boys wore suspenders and bow ties.

Freddy was spinning the ring bearer pillow over his head. Ivy threw the remainder of her rose petals at Constance and Thomas as they waltzed. The twins were passing out wedding wands with ribbons and bells attached.

So far, they hadn't clocked anyone.

Hollie flattened a hand to his chest, toying with his suit tie. "You don't think Freddy had a frog under the ring pillow, do you?"

Ha. Probably. "I wouldn't put it past him."

"We're almost done with the wedding events."

"You did it," he emphasized as he'd done for countless years. How long before she believed him?

She paused for a moment, their bodies moving in time together as her hand drifted back to his open palm. As the music slowed, she laid her head on his chest. "We've been a good team for so long. I've been worrying lately that we can't do this separately. That dividing forces will mean the collapse of everything." She tipped her face up to meet his gaze squarely, her eyes somber. "We've made a mess of things, haven't we?"

A depressing notion, but there was also a glimmer of hope in what she'd said. She was thinking about the downside to leaving. He searched for the right words to keep this window of opportunity open without spooking her.

Jacob let the music fill the void for a few beats as he waltzed them past the bride and groom. Constance's face was bright as she planted a kiss on Thomas's cheek. He tapped his hand over his heart twice while he smiled. Little Ivy twirled around them, pretending to be a fairy, which pulled laughter from the bride and groom.

That's what life should look like. Why hadn't he been able to make that happen for them? The weight of failure stole the air from his lungs.

His hands clenched tighter, as if he could hold on to her, will her not to leave. How often he'd done that same thing while sitting beside her during chemo treatments. "I just want to do a better job at protecting you."

"I don't think it's possible to protect anyone from life. Look at the hand those children have been dealt." Her face tipped toward the Hudson siblings, all four now holding hands and dancing in a circle around the bride and groom.

A well of emotion clogged Jacob's throat. Sometimes the Top Dog magic was so intensely sweet that it hurt. "Constance and Thomas look taken with them. I know they're older, but maybe…"

"Maybe…" Shadows crossed her face, threatening to steal this pocket of time.

He pressed a finger to her lips. "You don't have to finish that sentence or even that thought."

"What do you want from me, Jacob?"

"I just want you to dance with me."

An hour later, Hollie's body was still humming from being in Jacob's arms, hungry for this fairy-tale wedding reception to end so they could go back to their quarters together.

Since Ashlynn and Charlotte had overseen the execution, Hollie felt relief as she sat down at one of the pink-cloth-covered reception tables. Miniature castles with billowing arches made of candles washed the blush tablecloth in an otherworldly glow. White roses framed the castle figurine.

Hollie leaned forward in her cloth-draped chair, pushing chocolate-dipped fruit around on the tiny crystal dish between slices of brie. She'd taste-tested everything served at these weddings, but it seemed life always moved too fast for her to sit down and enjoy the party food all at once at an event.

Her mind skated back to the burger joint night with Jacob, so perfect.

She had all the time in the world to eat now, and yet her appetite was nowhere to be found. She wasn't even tempted by the tenderloin carving station or the bruschetta. She just continued to push a chunk of pineapple around her plate.

Shawna stepped up to the small table, carrying a plate and a drink. She wore a little black dress borrowed from Hollie, her pink streak of hair clipped back with a pearl-encrusted comb. "Is this seat taken?"

"It's all yours." She waved toward the chair across from her.

"Thanks." Shawna sat, placing her plate with a slice of wedding cake alongside her glass of sparkling water. "The kids are having such fun, I feel like I can relax for a minute."

"Of course you should. Who knows when the roads will open back up? You may be stuck here for a while, so you'd better fortify yourself." Hollie speared the chocolate-covered pineapple chunk and gestured toward Freddy chatting up the waitstaff serving cake. "I wonder if he's telling her that people in the wedding party are his parents."

Jacob strode up behind the children and helped them choose slices—finding the ones with the most frosting. Her heart squeezed in her chest.

Shawna rested her chin in her hand. "I can understand why they don't share the real story, why Elliot can't even bear to talk to other people at all."

"What happened?" she found herself blurting out in spite of how hard she'd worked to protect herself with a bit of distance. "If it's alright that I ask."

"It was in all the papers six months ago. I'm just surprised no one here has mentioned it." She sipped her water, then set her glass down carefully. "They were with their parents at a gas station, coming back from a camping trip. Someone held the cashier at gunpoint. The getaway turned ugly, and shots were fired. Their dad and mom were outside of the vehicle. Their dad died trying to protect their mom. The children were inside the car and saw the aftermath."

Hollie was shocked silent for four heartbeats. Her gaze gravitated to the Hudson children, all four of them now sitting with their backs against a wall, with Jake right there beside them as they ate cake. His grown-up-sized boots looked so incongruous and yet so sweet beside those four pairs of little kid shoes. "And there was no one for them? No family?"

Shaking her head, Shawna pressed a fork through the elderberry cream filling layered in the slice of wedding cake. "Two of their grandparents had passed, and the other two are much older, in assisted living, so they aren't able to take in four small children. There's only one other relative, an uncle on their dad's side. He is a bachelor who works on oil rigs, with a fiancée who has no interest in taking on the children. The grandparents send cards every now and again. But that's it."

How could four kids, so deeply loved, end up this alone? There were no simple answers. Splitting them up would be devastating. "I keep hoping that the coverage from these past two weeks will help."

Shawna set aside her fork with a weary sigh. "It could help children in the system overall, but it's doubtful anything could happen in time for these kids to find a home together. It's a process and it takes so long. Getting cleared to foster. Then being cleared to adopt. Not many will go through all of that to take in four children at once."

"You're right about the challenges, of course."

Hollie tossed aside her twisted napkin, heartsick. "I didn't mean to oversimplify."

The sound of childish laughter twined through the music and teased her ears, reminding her of JJ. He'd just started those baby giggles right before he returned to his birth mother.

It was tough to let go of those fairy-tale dreams, even as an adult. But the real world was not fantasy material, and too often, the innocent paid the highest price.

Hollie straightened in her seat, certain of what she needed to do even though Jacob would object. Angling forward, she pushed aside her plate, rested her elbows on the table and leaned closer to Shawna. "I have a favor to ask, and it's a big one." She steeled herself, gathering her courage because she needed to know in order to move forward. "I have to find out if the little boy we adopted—if JJ—is happy and safe."

Chapter Thirteen

The next morning, the rain had let up, at least for a moment. Surveying the aftermath of the storm, Jacob shaded his eyes from the sun peeking through a patch of sky, even though the day was still overcast. Some branches had been loosed from their trees, and frogs croaked happily from nestled ferns.

And Jacob intended to use that time to work some energy out of the Hudson kids while Hollie met with Allegra and Simon to finalize their modified plans for their wedding.

The final event.

He had parked himself in front of the garden

gate so no one—including Freddy—could escape without him noticing. Jacob sat in an Adirondack chair with his legs extended to brace against the gate post, his tablet on his knees so he could plow through work emails.

The boys were under a blanket fort draped over the patio table and four chairs—more like a blanket fortress. Shawna was sitting under a sprawling oak with Ivy, a quilt spread on the grass as they played with Hollie's old dolls. The kitten they'd rescued from the van engine was curled up asleep by Ivy's knee, having gotten an all clear from the vet tech they kept on staff. The thick branches from the ancient oak cast dappled shadows over the garden.

Why hadn't he thought to hang a tire swing from that tree? The space called for it in a way he hadn't noticed before, and he could imagine the giggles that swing would draw from the Hudson kids.

A motion in his peripheral view drew his attention. The tent flap "door" to the fort swung wide. Freddy crawled out, stood, and stretched as he took off his backwards ball cap. Toying with the well-worn hat, Freddy walked over to Jacob. His shoulders sagged in his superhero T-shirt.

Jacob set aside his tablet on the nearby patio

table beside his still-warm mug of black coffee. "What do you need, buddy?"

"Nothing. I'm just tired of being in the fort." He scuffed the toes of his tennis shoes against the patio stones. "Phillip and Elliot are doing their twin thing."

"Twin thing?"

Freddy nodded gravely, putting his ball cap back on his messy hair. "My mom used to say that twins have a special bond, and the rest of the world just fades away. Poof."

He unfurled his fists like releasing dust.

The way Freddy's shoulders still sagged downward signaled such loneliness. Jacob took a sip of his coffee, thinking for a moment on what he could offer the boy...

Jacob set aside his mug. "Would you like to come see the butterfly house?"

Freddy's eyes sparked with reluctant interest. "Sure. Uh, but what's a butterfly house? Is it close? I'm not supposed to leave Ms. Shawna. I'm already out of second chances."

"The butterfly house is right here in the garden. I gave it to Hollie for her last birthday." He'd hoped that their relationship would be like one of those caterpillars, just waiting to change into something beautiful again.

Jacob walked him over to the tiny yellow house on a post, tucked in with a cluster of wildflowers.

Freddy frowned, crossing his arms. "I thought that was a bird house."

Stooping slightly, Jacob pointed through the wildflowers that still held heavy raindrops on their brightly colored petals "Do you see the long slits there?" He pointed to the three thin rectangular cutouts.

Freddy stood on his tiptoes, inching closer to the gray stone edging. "Uh-huh."

"Well, those are different than the round hole you would normally see for a bird to go inside. In fact, these are narrower to protect the cocoons and caterpillars until they're ready to fly." Jacob tucked his two thumbs together, making a butterfly shape with his hands. Freddy's brow scrunched, a look Jacob was starting to recognize as interested.

He put a finger in the air, pointing to a phantom light bulb above his head. Freddy's gap-toothed grin was charming. "Kinda like how parents make sure we can't get out of the yard until we're old enough to be safe."

What an insightful comment. "I hadn't thought of it that way, but you're right."

Freddy looked back over his shoulder to where Shawna sat. A line of sadness seemed to part his lips. Then he inhaled sharply. "My dad kept us safe."

"I can see that."

"Like this one day, we were coming home from camping…" He skimmed a finger along the post of the butterfly house, tracing painted flowers. Freddy's eyes did not rise to meet him. Instead, they were trained in front of him. "We had a new puppy, and dad let us take her. We stopped at the gas station for a bathroom break and snacks."

"Yes, and what happened next?"

"Dad was pumping gas, so he kept an eye on our puppy, Roxy, while we went inside. Mom said we didn't even have to get healthy stuff if we didn't want. So I got potato chips. Ivy wanted cotton candy. Phillip picked a candy bar. And Elliot chose his favorite—gummy bears."

Jacob stayed silent, letting the boy find his way through the memory, sensing that the details were important. Specifics amplified during pivotal times.

"We started walking back to the car, and there were these firecrackers going off. I mean, I thought that's what they were." Freddy sent him a sidelong look. "I turned around to look, and it was really a guy with a gun. He was trying to steal money from the girl at the cash register."

A cold knot settled in Jacob's gut. Hollie had shared the basics of what she'd learned on the Hudson parents' death, but hearing it from Freddy was beyond gut-wrenching. No wonder the boy had made up fantasies about what happened to his parents. The truth was too terrible to bear.

"Mom shouted really loud to Dad. I can't remember what she said. I wish I could. Dad picked up Ivy and grabbed my arm. Mom was tugging Phillip and Elliot." Words continued to spill from Freddy, the pace faster and faster with each syllable.

Freddy's fingers skimmed up to outline the openings in the butterfly house. "Dad put me in the car fast, and I dropped my bag of potato chips. Ivy was crying so loud she got the hiccups." He paused for three shallow breaths before continuing. "Mom sorta tripped, and Dad went to help her because she was really hurt. He shouted for us to stay down on the floor of the car. Not to look."

Freddy's voice reminded him of a tree cracking under the weight of too much winter snow. For so many heartbeats, Jacob held his breath, watching as Freddy tried to steady himself. A shuddering went through the boy as silence lingered while Freddy traced a painted flower on the butterfly house, pausing on the petal of the daisy.

Eyes closed, Freddy continued, his voice almost a whisper, "I did what he said. And I kept saying it over and over again to my brothers and my sister. But Elliot climbed up on the seat, holding on to Roxy. He looked out the window."

All the Top Dog experiences in the world couldn't prepare him for a conversation like this. He snuck a glance at Shawna, in need of backup on every level, but she was engrossed in playing dolls with Ivy. He would have motioned for her to join them, but he also didn't want to stop the cathartic flow that Freddy seemed to need. Deeply. So Jacob listened and waited, his breath held while the child gathered his thoughts.

Freddy worked a finger through one of the openings in the butterfly house. "Dad kept us safe. But there was nobody to keep Mom and Dad safe."

Jacob rested a careful hand on the little boy's shoulder. Tapping into what little he knew from Top Dog workshops about healing relationships, Jacob rolled out whatever he could think of to comfort Freddy. And he liked to hope he did a better job comforting Freddy than he had with Patsy the night of Lonnie's heart attack. Yet his efforts sounded hollow in his ears, and not nearly the kind of support the kid deserved after all he'd been through.

Jacob thought his heart was beyond breaking anymore, too full of scar tissue and brick walls. He was wrong. This little boy had knocked down those barriers, revealing what Jacob should have realized all along.

He didn't have anything left inside him to give to another person, not a child and most certainly not his wife. He couldn't play at some sort of half-in/half-out version of a relationship with Hollie.

Their marriage was truly and completely over.

Hollie had been about to burst with excitement all evening long, waiting for a moment alone with Jacob to tell him about her conversation with Shawna at the princess-style wedding reception.

She paced around their bedroom suite. Anticipation powered her steps as she checked the fireplace, the mugs of tea on the coffee table, the floral arrangement by the bed, leftovers from one of the weddings. The shower echoed from the master bathroom, and she considered just stepping into the stall to surprise him. But if she did, there wasn't a chance they would talk for a while. Besides, he'd been so silent since his conversation with Freddy. What had they spoken about? She needed to remember to ask him.

Maybe he was just tired, perhaps? Frustrated over all the rain?

No matter. She would find out later. She was certain his mood would lift when she told him her news. Even if he might object initially, surely he would be happy when he saw how happy it made her to have the report to look forward to.

And she hoped—truly hoped—that positive news about JJ would help her heal. She needed that. She'd been so devastated about the loss of the boy for so long. At least hearing that he was happy, loved, could bring her weary heart some peace.

It was her hope it could do the same for Jacob. That a path to news of JJ could part the clouds in their storm. Hollie fidgeted with a lock of hair, picking at the ends in an unsuccessful effort to quell her heartfelt anticipation.

The echo of the shower stopped, and less than a minute later, Jacob came out, rubbing his hair dry with a towel, wearing dark gray sweatpants and nothing else. The sight of his hard muscled chest and broad shoulders sent a thrill through her. And the way his sweats hung low on his hips…

Once they finished talking, she looked forward to exploring every inch of him in celebration of something positive. He'd been so emphatic about them giving things another go, a thought she had so often discounted. Fear and pain from the past had guided that refusal to try. Today she wondered if perhaps he could be right on that. Sure, there were times when he seemed rather emotionless about it all, but that didn't mean things couldn't change down the road.

It wasn't as if they were starting from scratch. They shared so much history. They shared a bond in the child they'd loved. In her mind's eye, she saw still frames of their past: JJ sleeping in Jacob's arms, laughter as they picked out cowboy-themed onesies. A small memory that fueled her even now. Maybe it always would push her forward.

She cupped her mug of tea to keep her hands occupied so she could share her news before toppling him onto the bed. "Jacob, I've got something to tell you."

"Can it wait?" He tossed the towel into the hamper, then combed his hand through his hair to smooth it down. "We need to talk first."

She bit her lip, her fingertips thrumming against the pink mug with gold writing that read, *I woof you*.

"But it's really amazing. I think you're going to want to hear. I'm not sure I can contain myself."

His shoulders slumped, and he dropped into a

chair by the fireplace. "What's it about? Something for tomorrow? The weather's looking clear."

"No, it has nothing to do with work or even the weather." Setting side her mug, she took his hands and squeezed, her eyes roving his strong jaw. Preparing herself for his reaction to the news, she took a breath, grounding her nerves. A tremor of excitement was washing through her so strongly, she didn't want to spill her cinnamon, clove and orange peel tea on her lap.

"I think I've found a way for us to get an update on JJ."

His head snapped back as if he'd been punched. He tugged his hands from her grip.

"Jacob, this is good news if it pans out." Hollie couldn't stop the hopeful smile that cut across her face. She reached for him again, needing to connect.

Apparently, he didn't feel the same since he crossed his arms.

"Hollie, we've been over this. He's gone." His voice cracked on the last word.

His hands clenched, knuckles going white with an anxiety she understood. If anything, that spurred her on. He needed hope. And so did she.

She skimmed her hand along his fist, hoping to soothe him into hearing her and processing this great news. She tried to catch his eye, but his gaze was trained on a spot on the carpet ahead of them.

Sensing his confusion, she knew she needed to clarify the path forward. But she had to believe they still wanted the same things. Hadn't he spent the last two weeks showing her they could still be a team? "I spoke to Shawna, and she gave me the names of some organizations that might be able to help—all completely legal. It's unlikely we'd be able to see him, but they would reach out to his birth mother."

"We've already tried that, and she refused." Every muscle in Jacob's body transformed from relaxed to rigid, an echo of the mountains to their east.

"Shawna said that's not unusual initially, particularly if the request isn't handled in a delicate enough manner." Hollie reached into her pocket for her phone. When the phone came to life at her touch, she let herself pause on her recently restored lock screen photo taken last summer—a picture of her, Jacob and JJ underneath the oak tree at the front of the lodge. The image filled her chest with hope, longing. "She forwarded me the names of people in the system to contact, people she trusts. We can try again..."

"I can't do that." His tone had the same quality of winter's first frost—abrupt and arresting.

His words stopped her cold. "What did you say?"

"I cannot go that path again." The white of his knuckles intensified. Hard lines sculpted his body, matching the far-off look in his eyes.

His face was so stony, so closed, she barely recognized him.

"Why not? The worst they can say is no."

His eyes fluttered shut for a moment. He blinked them open, a sigh expanding his muscled chest. For the first time since he sat down, he turned to meet her stare.

Adam's apple bobbing and voice low, he said, "I'm done, Hollie."

"Done being JJ's father? How can you say that?" How had they reversed roles on this? For so long he'd pushed her to try for adoption again, to not let what happened with JJ cripple her ability to love. But now, just when she'd found hope again, he seemed to have lost his. "I will always be JJ's mother. Always. Even if I never see him again, if I never get any update on him, I'm still his mom, and I won't stop doing whatever I can to—"

His jaw flexed, anger and hurt creasing the corners of his eyes. "Whatever you can to…do what?

We aren't going to get him back. There's nothing more we can do for him."

How could he just give up? She'd thought he would be excited. Or at the very least that he would be relieved. What was going on with his defeatist attitude?

She shook her head, heartbeat thundering in her ears. A rasp scratched at her throat as she spoke. "There's always more."

"His birth mother knows how to reach us if she chooses. Our lawyer made sure our contact information will be available to JJ when he turns eighteen. So going down this path doesn't accomplish anything for him."

The blood chilled in her veins. The world became muffled.

How could he feel so closed off to the possibilities that Shawna had opened up for them? Hollie picked her tea mug back up, desperate for the warmth as she cupped her hands around the base. A lump rose that threatened to bring tears. She swallowed, the pain of losing JJ and the distance with Jacob heavy in her body.

Holding her mug tighter, she looked at her husband, searching for some hint of a way to get through to him. All his muscles were tensed. Pain cut through his mouth, compressing his plump lips into a thin line. His eyes, though, were anything but still. They were on fire with grief, anger, hurt. He was immovable.

Desperate to divert this runaway train discussion, she asked, "What did you want to tell me when you came out of the shower?"

He plowed his fingers through his damp hair. "It doesn't matter anymore."

Hollie steeled her resolve. She was committed to stitching this wound. "If it's important to you, then it matters to me."

Standing, he headed toward the patio doors. "It's not important now. I'm going to clean up the blanket fort."

She set aside her mug and raced to catch him. She touched his arm, wanting to halt the conversation that was spinning out of control far too fast. Needing to stop him from pulling further away, because she sensed that if he went through that door, there would be no turning back for them. "How can you just walk out in the middle of the first meaningful conversation we've had in far too long? You have to know that was a part of what started our problems."

What had happened to her husband? Because this man was like a stranger, looking at her with such cold distance in his eyes, with a disconnect she couldn't recall ever seeing before. Had it been there when he'd walked in the door and she'd been too full of her own news to see it? She swallowed hard. Waiting. Fearing.

"I'm sorry I haven't communicated like a grade-A graduate from the Top Dog Dude Ranch," he said tightly. "So I'll try to be clearer. You're not willing to go forward, and I can't go back. I've finally come to realize that you're right. Our marriage is over."

Chapter Fourteen

The afternoon skies were cloudless. The roads leaving the ranch were clear. And the two week wedding extravaganza was coming to an end.

Appropriate, really, since his marriage was drawing to a close.

With the sun beating down to steam away all moisture from the past storms, Jacob closed the engine of the minivan. Even knowing it was in perfect working order, he couldn't help but check again before the Hudson kids loaded up to leave.

The argument with Hollie had been brutal. He'd still been reeling from Freddy's revelation about his parents' murder when Hollie had unleashed her plan to get an update on JJ. Jacob hadn't even been able to imagine opening himself up to the possibility of any more pain. He'd laid his heart out there for Hollie these past weeks, for the Hudson kids, too.

And now, he had to accept he couldn't go on.

He was done.

It wasn't fair to her to continue this way when they had too much shared heartache. He wanted to give her more than he was able. Asking her to settle for less wasn't fair to her. But he'd known immediately when she'd announced her plan to check on JJ that he couldn't go along with what she wanted. He wouldn't stand in her way of pursuing something so important to her, but he also couldn't join her in that quest when his heart was so raw. He just had to get through these goodbyes, and then he would move on with his life. Alone.

Ivy peeped up at him, her eyes appearing wider thanks to her glasses. Her tiny tiara from the wedding was perched along the top of her French braid. "Thank you for a very wonderful vacation."

"You're welcome, princess. Thank you for being such a great flower girl for Mr. Thomas and Mrs. Constance."

She gestured for him to lean down, and for an

instant, he thought she was going to kiss him on the cheek.

Then she whispered, "Tell Mrs. Hollie that I will take good care of her dolls."

His heart squeezed in his chest. "I sure will. She would have been here to say goodbye, but she's at work."

Which, loosely translated, meant that Hollie was avoiding him since their argument. Which was probably for the best. He'd tried everything he could think of these past weeks, and each attempt only ended up making them hurt worse.

Phillip collected a few more acorns, stuffing them in his pockets before clambering up into the van. Elliot cradled the kitten, whispering his farewells, then passing Porkchop to Jacob.

Freddy wouldn't even say goodbye. He was already in the van, slumped in a seat with his arms crossed and his ball cap pulled low over his eyes.

As much as Jacob didn't want any part of Shawna and Hollie's plan to get information about JJ, Jacob also didn't want to take out his bad mood on the kids. That wasn't fair.

Cradling Porkchop in one hand, he pulled a Top Dog Dude Ranch ball cap from his back pocket and strode over to the driver's side door. Shawna was standing outside the transport van, looking at her phone, double-checking the map.

He held out the gift. "Could you make sure Freddy gets this? I was going to give it to him when we said goodbye, but he's, uh, napping."

"Goodbyes are difficult for him." She took the hat from him, tucking it under one arm.

"That's understandable." He glanced at the kid through the window, wishing there was more he could do.

Shawna gestured to the expanse of Top Dog Dude Ranch while her eyes brightened in the spring sunshine. "Thank you again, to you and Hollie both."

"We're just doing our best to provide the Top Dog experience." He hoped she would get the message that he didn't want to chitchat.

She put away her phone. "No, it was more than that. You opened your home to us, shared your personal space. You—this place—have made an impression on these children that they'll carry with them forever."

"Those rug rats definitely made an impression on us as well." He would never forget them, never stop wondering what happened to them and hoping they landed the very best of the best out of life. He couldn't check up on them any more than he could check up on JJ. He only had so much left inside him to give. Not nearly enough.

His gut knotted all over again.

Shawna looked toward her small charges, then back at him. "Thank you most for the last couple of days and making the rain delay so special. Building a blanket fort. Playing with dolls. Making ice cream. Learning about butterfly houses. All of those everyday normal things that people take for granted. Those simple, quiet moments are healing."

He scratched the back of his neck, drawn into the conversation in spite of himself. "Well, I'm not so sure about that. While I was showing Freddy the butterfly house, he told me about the day his parents died. It didn't sound like a story. All his other tales had a positive spin. This was...tragic."

"What did he tell you?"

Jacob rubbed a hand over the ache in his chest. "He said his parents were shot during a robbery at a gas station. He said his parents died protecting them."

Shawna nodded. "That is correct."

He'd thought as much, and yet having the confirmation made the news devastating all over again.

"For a child to see..." He shook his head. "He

remembered so many details, down to what snacks they bought. Even the name of their new puppy in the car."

"When the police arrived, Elliot was talking to the puppy. That's how the cops got the details on what happened. Called for child services for the kids. And notified the shelter about the puppy." She traced the toe of her ankle boots through the soft soil. "They've been through such trauma. We have counselors on staff. We're trying our best."

"I wish we were in a position to…" He looked down. "Hollie and I aren't together anymore. So if you pursue her question about the child we were adopting, there's no need to share the information with me."

Shawna's eyebrows shot up. "I'm sorry to hear that about you and Hollie."

"There's no need to burden you with the details. I just feel like I need to explain why we aren't begging to keep those amazing kids."

"Don't apologize. No one should be pressured or guilted into adopting. That does a potentially catastrophic disservice to the parents and the children."

"Thank you." He couldn't help but wonder how his and Hollie's adoption experience would have turned out had Shawna been at the helm.

All a moot point now.

He opened the driver's side door for Shawna, waving her in. "Drive safely."

"Of course." Shawna settled in behind the wheel, waving as he closed the door and thumped the roof.

And then he realized the gesture wasn't addressed to him. Her attention was focused somewhere behind him. He looked over his shoulder to find Hollie standing on the lodge steps. Even from twenty yards away, he could see her mood matched his. Yet she lifted a hand, waving goodbye to the children.

Tucking Porkchop closer to his chest, Jacob scratched behind the animal's soft ears. He couldn't help but wonder how long it would take for the kitten's purr to translate into much-needed healing.

Hollie knew she should be helping the staff set up for Allegra and Simon's wedding. She'd never been one to shirk work.

But between her fight with Jacob and seeing the Hudson kids leave, she didn't trust herself to keep her emotions in check just yet.

At least this one last wedding was less formal than the others. Allegra and Simon had been emphatic that their down-to-earth styles be reflected. Most of what their parents had planned was scrapped. Instead, the couple said their vows in front of the waterfall...which had been the plan for Constance's Cinderella ceremony. Hollie had recycled what she could, while giving it all an eco-adventure vibe that reflected the pair's love of nature.

Allegra's eucalyptus flower crown complemented the green garlands she and Ashlynn strung on stylized wooden arches that framed the seating area. Prisms in the shape of small prisms hung from the boughs of trees that provided shade for the attendees. Dressed in clay earth tones, Simon walked shoulder to shoulder with his bride and was met by claps and whistles from all of the gathered family—not a single argument broke out.

Now the reception was in full swing on the lodge grounds. Dinner was set up on reclaimed wood planks. Raise the Woof was playing retro rock with a scenic mountain backdrop.

There was nothing left for her to do.

She'd struggled to make polite conversation. So she'd removed herself from the crowd to review photo proofs Milo had sent her. Sitting on a boulder near a mountain ledge, a couple dozen yards from the reception, she swiped through the images.

On the bridge in their wedding gear.

Riding on the horse together.

Dancing the Scottish reel.

Kissing in their garden? Where had Milo been lurking? Thank goodness they'd gone inside.

She swiped again, her hand slowing as she came to the most moving images of all. Jacob, Freddy and the twins brushing Ziggy. Hollie reading with Ivy.

Jacob's arm around Hollie as they watched the children horseback riding.

When she looked at the photos, she not only saw that pain, but she also saw the love between them. Love as vibrant as in any of those wedding photos of other couples.

Couples who hadn't been through the pain that life had waiting in the wings. But as fast as that thought swelled through her, she flinched at the bitterness. When had she let all those scars on her heart tarnish her view of even the joys life had to offer?

Resting her phone on her knee, she stared out into the stillness of the woods, the mountains and valleys of home. A pebble glinted beside her, and Hollie picked it up, playing with the smooth edges. An understanding blossomed in her chest as vibrant as any spring flower.

She didn't know where the knowledge came from, but maybe she'd just needed the quiet time to reflect after the nonstop mayhem of the last two weeks. She wanted Jacob to have the family she believed he'd been denied because of her. After her cancer battle, she'd tried to make him happy by pushing him toward adoption, certain he'd deserved a family. Yet her pushing had only brought him pain.

She'd thought learning about JJ would somehow ease that for them both, but she'd been so very wrong.

And for the first time in far too long, she let herself truly look at her husband, her heart open. Allowing herself to feel, to risk pain. She saw his love for her.

Even if she shared a dozen pictures and updates on JJ, that wouldn't heal the pain—hers or his. Because maybe the deepest ache they were experiencing was for each other.

It was time she acknowledged that her love for her husband had never died. Cutting him out of her life wasn't going to protect her from hurt. Losing him would leave a void in her life she could never hope to fill.

He'd stolen her heart as a teenager, and he held it still. She didn't know what their future had in store for them, but then, no one did. It was time for them to find a way to healing—together. She clutched her phone tightly with one hand as if afraid that a loose grip would lessen her chances.

Tendrils of a plan began to form as she started scrolling through her recent messages. Once she landed on Milo's name, she drew in a deep breath of mountain air.

She'd thought Milo's photos would launch a future for the ranch and the children, not even entertaining the notion there could be something in his photographic genius for her. For her marriage.

But now, finally, she was ready to ask, to accept the aid, beauty, the magical healing love that Moonlight Ridge had in store for her and for Jacob. Her thumbs flew over the keyboard.

Milo, I need your help…

Three hours later, Jacob steered his pickup truck along the dirt road leading to the area designated as the ranch's makeshift drive-in movie theater. A mountainside had been smoothed out like a screen, with a sprawling grassy area in front for picnic blankets.

And it was empty.

So why had Hollie asked him to meet her here?

The crisp air scented with pine and star jasmine

swirled through his open windows, awakening his senses. Even as he drove toward the mountainside, faint lights and musical notes from Allegra and Simon's reception echoed like the edge of a whisper. Headlights from his truck beamed across the open field, landing on a lone figure sitting on a quilt.

Hollie.

He was wary about seeing her again after what happened between them. And no doubt, he had regrets about the way he'd ended things. He was still too numb to have sorted through the hurt of the fight, but he knew he couldn't refuse her when she wanted to see him. No matter what the future held, they were still husband and wife right now, with so much shared history.

He pulled his truck alongside her, put it into Park, and turned off the engine. Stepping out, he took in the sight of her in jeans and a simple sweatshirt she'd changed into after leaving the reception. Bandit was curled up asleep on the quilt, keeping her company.

Jacob tugged on his jacket to guard against the chill in the breeze that stirred Hollie's hair. "What's going on? Is everything okay?"

Hollie extended her hand to him. "It's a surprise. Come sit with me. Don't say a word. Just watch…"

He knew she wouldn't have news about JJ yet, and he trusted her not to share that with him when he'd told her that updates like that would be too painful.

Confused, but unable to deny her—when had he ever been able to tell her no?—he stretched out beside her on the heirloom quilt. A wedding gift from one of her friends, he recalled. The pattern was called "wedding ring."

As if he needed any more scores on his heart today.

Hollie pulled out her tablet and typed quickly. At her command, the movie projector light splashed across the mountainside. No sound.

Just…photos?

His breath caught at the sight of them together so many years ago, a memory long forgotten of them at the ice-cream shop where she'd worked. They were so young. So in love they could hardly keep their eyes off one another. And then, one after the other, the pictures of their lives together scrolled through—dating, wedding, growing the Top Dog Dude Ranch. Even JJ.

Their relationship together played out in front of him until he realized his eyes were wet with tears. Hollie's hand slid into his and squeezed. He felt the love flow from her. But he also felt the support.

The anchor of her beside him. Her strength. Her steadiness.

Things he'd never let himself fully experience before. He'd been too busy trying to be the strong one. Trying to give her everything she'd ever needed. He hadn't seen that he needed her, too. "Thank you for this. It's...beautiful."

Tears glistened in the corner of Hollie's eyes as she swallowed twice before speaking. "Our life together is beautiful, isn't it? I'm sorry I lost sight of that. Can you forgive me for pushing you away?"

Of course he could. With the beautiful images of their life together still fresh in his mind, he wondered how he ever could have lost sight of that connection they'd shared. He'd been derailed for a time.

But never again. Hollie was the love of his life. And he now—finally—saw and believed that he was the love of her life as well.

Jacob squeezed her hand back, then hauled her into his arms, holding her close and whispering into her hair. "You've got nothing to apologize for. I should have shared my grief with you. I'm so very sorry for closing down, for shutting you out."

Hollie held him tight, her face buried in his shirt. "I understand you've always tried to protect me."

Easing away, he smoothed her hair from her face, needing to see her eyes as they sat side by side. "You were going through so much physically, I didn't want to add to your burden. I didn't grasp that I was making things worse by keeping everything inside since you undoubtedly saw through me."

She tipped her head against his shoulder. "It means a lot to hear you open up now."

Was it enough? He wasn't going to assume or settle. He was going to keep working. Because by some miracle, this incredible woman was giving him a second chance.

And he loved her. Not just in some benign way that had dulled over time. Time had actually strengthened his love for this woman. With every ounce of his being, he was committed to her. Hollie was his soul mate, the woman of his dreams, yesterday and tomorrow.

Images of their life together kept splashing across the mountainside, the picture montage reflected in her eyes.

In his heart.

"Hollie, I want us to grow a partnership, not just in business but in our relationship. I hate that we lost sight of that along the way." He traced her knuckles with his thumb, up one hill and down the next valley, savoring the smooth feel of her, the nuances of her body.

"I want that, too. I know there has been a lot of pain for both of us, and work offered a distraction. Now I'm wondering if maybe that was a bad thing." She flattened her palms against his chest. "Because somehow, I stopped telling you—showing you—how very much I love you."

"Hollie, I should be telling you that first. Because I do love you, so deeply. Always."

"You chased me when we first met. Well, now I'm chasing you. Get used to it," she said, grinning. Then she leaned forward on her knees to kiss him. Lingering.

The joy of having her in his arms again was… everything. He wanted to hold her there, hold on to this moment. But they had more to settle. They couldn't afford to lose themselves in their connection when he needed to shore up their bond so they could go the distance together. Forever.

He eased back, shifting her onto his lap, holding her. "You're not the only one who's been thinking. Seeing the couples these past two weeks has reminded me that relationships come in many shapes. And every single one of those requires attention to the relationship."

Hollie laughed softly. "Things did seem to turn around for us on all those wedding crasher dates."

"You have a point." He traced her lips with a finger, then skimmed his mouth over hers. "I'm not delusional enough, though, to think that's all we need to keep things on track."

"What do you mean?" She caressed his cheek, hope in her gaze.

"Lonnie and I had an interesting conversation before he got sick…" Thank goodness he'd been released from the hospital, with a positive report and a detailed plan from the hospital's dietician. "He suggested we consider counseling."

His shoulders tensed as he waited for her verdict, praying she was on board and not defensive. He so badly wanted things to work and was committed to trying whatever it took to make forever happen.

"I'm listening…" She sketched her fingertips along his collar bones, her gaze steady on his.

Drawing in a deep breath of mountain home air, he willed his thoughts to align. He'd given countless speeches here at the ranch, but this was different. The words had to be just right. She deserved the fairy tale. She deserved…everything.

So he abandoned his prepared speech and spoke from the heart.

"I think we lured ourselves into believing that this place really did have some kind of magic. But relationships—life—is more complicated than that. The magic comes from the connections. The animals and the land help nudge that along. But the healing? That comes from our guests' openness to help themselves and help each other."

"You've given this a lot of thought."

"Well, I have some time to make up for in pushing down everything going on in here." He tapped his chest, right over his heart.

She clasped his hands in hers and leaned into him. "I'm completely open to counseling. I want us to heal, as a couple."

A sigh of relief shuddered through him. "I'm so glad to hear that."

She arched up to skim her mouth against his for a moment before she continued, "I need you to understand that I want our family to include children. I truly do. But I'm scared. And what happens if that doesn't come together? It's been difficult for me knowing I'm keeping you from having a family."

He was scared, too. But he was more afraid of living his life without her. "Hollie, we already are a family. You and I. This home of ours and all our menagerie of empathic, quirky animals. This is our beautiful life." He gestured to the mountain-side screen. "As you so eloquently showed me."

Her shaky sigh revealed just how nervous she'd been. He hoped he never gave her cause to doubt him again.

"Oh, Jacob," she breathed against his mouth. "I'm so glad you saw what I see now when I look at those photos. And I look forward to all the beautiful ones we'll be adding for years to come."

"Hollie O'Brien, I promise to love, honor and cherish you all the days of my life."

"Jacob O'Brien—" she took his face in her hands "—I will love you, honor you and cherish you for as long as there is breath in my body."

He sealed his mouth to hers. His promise in his kiss. He would have made love to her there under the stars, but Bandit nudged him on the elbow, reminding him of where they were.

Laughing, Jacob leaned back and ruffled the pup's ears. "Time for us to go home, my love."

Hollie stood alongside him. "There's nowhere on earth I'd rather be."

Epilogue

Six Months Later

Freddy held on to Ziggy's leash, standing very still while Mr. Milo took their photo.

"Squeeze in tighter," Mr. Milo said, his forehead turning a little pink in the afternoon sun. "Adults in the back, kids in the front. There are a lot of you. It's an important day, and we don't want to miss anyone."

That was for sure. Hollie and Jacob had just finished renewing their wedding vows on a mountainside—at one of the secret spots of the O'Brien family—and Freddy was excited to learn all the hideaways. Freddy wasn't an expert, but as he thought back to those weddings from six months ago, he was certain this was the best ceremony.

And the coolest thing of all? They were a part of this family now.

Freddy scooched closer to Ivy with Scottie, Phillip with Bandit, and Elliot holding their new beagle puppy, Ruby. Hollie and Jacob stood behind them in their wedding gear. Yeah, they were already married, but they'd said they wanted to renew their vows to celebrate their new beginning.

All the dogs had wreaths around their necks with flowers and ribbons that matched Hollie's bouquet. Her lacy white gown was one she'd worn when they got married the first time. Ivy wore a lacy white dress with pink cowgirl boots. Jacob wore jeans and a vest with a Stetson—just like him and Phillip and Elliot.

It didn't feel right to call Hollie and Jacob Mom and Dad. But they were more than Mr. and Mrs. O'Brien. So they'd decided Freddy and his siblings should call them Hollie and Jacob. If they came up with something later, that was okay, too. Hollie had said the most important thing was that they call each other a family.

He could still hardly believe they all got to live here at the Top Dog Dude Ranch forever. Right after they had left the ranch and got back to the group home, Hollie and Jacob had contacted Ms. Shawna about adopting them. All four of them. Even if Elliot never spoke again, they wanted them all—forever.

Since Hollie and Jacob had already gone through the process to become foster parents, it hadn't taken long before Freddy was helping his siblings pack to come back here. They had their own bedrooms, even though Elliot and Philip usually slept in one another's rooms anyway. Freddy liked having a space all his own, but it was even better to know that his brothers and sister were all safe.

And they were together. It seemed like Mom and Dad would be happy about that, and even though he missed them so much it still hurt, he liked knowing they would be proud of him for keeping his siblings together. And safe.

These days, they rode horses, went swimming. He'd even seen a foal being born. He was even okay with seeing Isabella every now and again when Mr. Thomas and Mrs. Connie came to visit. They'd decided to foster her. Isabella still got on his nerves, but at least she wasn't mean to Ivy anymore.

And best of all, Jacob was teaching him all

about expanding their butterfly garden. He said those butterflies were growing and changing into something beautiful, just like their lives. That good things could take time to come around.

Just like how it would take a while for the adoption to be complete—something about the courts and stuff making it official. But Hollie and Jacob assured them a zillion times a day that it was official in their hearts.

Ms. Shawna reminded them of that, too. She was working at the Top Dog Dude Ranch now. She was helping add more counselor stuff to the pack-tivities. Hollie and Jacob had also gotten a family counselor for all of them to see, to help them through all the changes. And to remember about the past sometimes, too. Talking about his feelings wasn't always easy, but he'd found once he had time to think about it, he felt better.

Miss Ashlynn was working at this ranch and not the other Top Dog Ranch after all. Hollie said she needed the extra help so she could spend more time with her family. Mr. Lonnie and Mrs. Patsy went to the other ranch to make sure everything there was being done "the Top Dog way" as Jacob liked to say.

The biggest change of all?

Elliot was talking to people. And talking. And talking. It was like he was pouring out all the words he'd stored up during that time he only spoke to animals. "Phillip, scoot over. You're on my toes. Am I standing in the right place? Can you see Ruby's flowers?"

Hollie leaned down and dropped a kiss on Elliot's head. "You and Ruby are absolutely perfect."

Jacob ruffled his hair. "That's right, champ."

This was going to be a really special picture to add to the gallery wall Hollie had made for them. It was packed with images of things they'd done together. Hollie had also made sure some of those photographs included their mom and dad. She'd found his mom's old social media profile, and he was so glad. Hollie said people posted their best pictures on social media.

She was smart that way.

Milo held up the camera. "Everyone ready? It's time. Say cheese."

That was Freddy's cue. The moment he'd been waiting for.

He tugged the chain that released a flurry of... butterflies.

They were lots of different sizes, fluttering all around and filling the air with all their colors. Jacob had built a big butterfly house the size of a little cabin. He'd said it made the perfect addition to the Top Dog experience.

Freddy was in charge. And he was pretty proud to see all those butterflies play their special part in today's photo.

Hollie said their family was like those butterflies, emerging from a cocoon to fill the world with beauty. He liked that. A lot. He had a book about butterflies now, and he searched for different ones in the woods and meadows the same way he'd looked for the birds that time when he'd first visited Top Dog Dude Ranch.

Only now, he didn't worry about finding them all. Good things took time, and he was okay with that.

Those butterflies had taught him something else. That once he'd stopped running, he'd found his way home again.

* * * * *

*Don't miss the next book in the
Top Dog Dude Ranch miniseries*

The Little Matchmaker

*Available June 2022 wherever
Harlequin Special Edition books
and ebooks are sold!*

COMING NEXT MONTH FROM

Ⓗ HARLEQUIN

SPECIAL EDITION

#2905 SUMMONING UP LOVE
Heart & Soul • by Synithia Williams
Vanessa Steele's retreated to her grandmother's beach house after she loses her job and her fiancé. When she finds out her grandmother has enlisted hunky Dion Livingston and his brothers to investigate suspicious paranormal activity, the intrepid reporter's skeptical of their motives. But her own investigation discovers that Dion's the real deal. And any supernatural energy? Pales compared to the electricity that erupts when the two of them are together...

#2906 A FORTUNE IN THE FAMILY
The Fortunes of Texas: The Wedding Gift • by Kathy Douglass
Contractor Josh Fortune is happy to be Kirby Harris's Mr. Fixit. Repairing the roof of Kirby's Perks is a cinch, but healing her heart is a trickier process. For three years the beautiful widow has been doing everything on her own, and she's afraid to let down her guard. She thinks Josh is too young, too carefree—and way too tempting for a mama who has to put her kids first...

#2907 SECOND-CHANCE SUMMER
Gallant Lake Stories • by Jo McNally
For golf pro Quinn Walker, Gallant Lake Resort's cheery yet determined manager, Julie Brown, is a thorn in his side. But the widowed single dad begrudgingly agrees to teach his sassy coworker the game he loves. As their lessons progress, Julie disarms Quinn in ways he can't explain...or ignore. A second chance at love is as rare as a hole in one. Can these rivals at work tee it up for love?

#2908 THE BOOKSHOP RESCUE
Furever Yours • by Rochelle Alers
Lucy Tucker never imagined how dramatically life would change once she started fostering Buttercup, a pregnant golden retriever. The biggest change? Growing a lot closer to Calum Ramsey. One romantic night later, and they're expecting a baby of their own! Stunned at first, steadfastly single Calum is now dutifully offering marriage. But Lucy wants the true-blue happy ending they both deserve.

#2909 A RANCH TO COME HOME TO
Forever, Texas • by Marie Ferrarella
Alan White Eagle hasn't returned to Forever since he left for college eight years ago. But when a drought threatens the town's existence, the irrigation engineer vows to help. An unlikely ally appears in the form of his childhood nemesis, Raegan. In fact, their attraction is challenging Alan's anti-romance workaholic facade. Will Alan's plan to save Forever's future end with a future with Raegan?

#2910 RELUCTANT ROOMMATES
Sierra's Web • by Tara Taylor Quinn
Living with a total stranger for twelve months is the only way Weston Thomas can claim possession of his Georgia family mansion. If not, the place goes to the dogs—seven rescue pups being looked after by Paige Martinson, his co-owner. But when chemistry deepens into more powerful emotions, is the accountant willing to bank on a future that was never in his long-term plans?

YOU CAN FIND MORE INFORMATION ON UPCOMING HARLEQUIN TITLES, FREE EXCERPTS AND MORE AT HARLEQUIN.COM.

HSECNM0322

Mariella Jacob was one of the world's premier bridal designers. One viral PR disaster later, she's trying to get her torpedoed career back on track in small-town Magnolia, North Carolina. With a second-hand store and a new business venture helping her friends turn the Wildflower Inn into a wedding venue, Mariella is finally putting at least one mistake behind her. Until that mistake—in the glowering, handsome form of Alex Ralsten—moves to Magnolia too...

Read on for a sneak preview of
Wedding Season,
the next book in USA TODAY bestselling author
Michelle Major's Carolina Girls series!

"You still don't belong here." Mariella crossed her arms over her chest, and Alex commanded himself not to notice her body, perfect as it was.

"That makes two of us, and yet here we are."

"I was here first," she muttered. He'd heard the argument before, but it didn't sway him.

"You're not running me off, Mariella. I needed a fresh start, and this is the place I've picked for my home."

"My plan was to leave the past behind me. You are a physical reminder of so many mistakes I've made."

"I can't say that upsets me too much," he lied. It didn't make sense, but he hated that he made her so uncomfortable. Hated even more that sometimes he'd purposely drive by her shop to get a glimpse of her through the picture window. Talk about a glutton for punishment.

She let out a low growl. "You are an infuriating man. Stubborn and callous. I don't even know if you have a heart."

"Funny." He kept his voice steady even as memories flooded him, making his head pound. "That's the rationale Amber gave me for why she cheated with your fiancé. My lack of emotions pushed her into his arms. What was his excuse?"

She looked out at the street for nearly a minute, and Alex wondered if she was even going to answer. He followed her gaze to the park across the street, situated in the center of the town. There were kids at the playground and several families walking dogs on the path that circled the perimeter. Magnolia was the perfect place to raise a family.

If a person had the heart to be that kind of a man—the type who married the woman he loved and set out to be a good husband and father. Alex wasn't cut out for a family, but he liked it in the small coastal town just the same.

"I was too committed to my job," she said suddenly and so quietly he almost missed it.

"Ironic since it was your job that introduced him to Amber."

"Yeah." She made a face. "This is what I'm talking about, Alex. A past I don't want to revisit."

"Then stay away from me, Mariella," he advised. "Because I'm not going anywhere."

"Then maybe I will," she said and walked away.

Don't miss
Wedding Season by Michelle Major,
available May 2022 wherever
HQN books and ebooks are sold.

HQNBooks.com

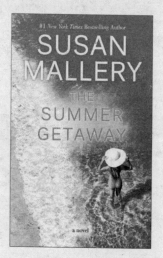

"Look." Quinn's eyes narrowed dangerously. "If this
game is that simple, why are you here? If anyone here
should feel like they're being punked, it's *me*. You
obviously expect to become magically competent at
a game you have no respect for without putting in any
of the work. I don't know what motivated you to take
lessons, but if you're not going to work at it, don't waste
my time."

Her whole body went still. Even her lungs seemed
to pause. She'd never been good at hearing criticism,
especially from men. And Quinn had just used a whole
bunch of trigger words. She could hear her mother's voice
in her head. *You never listen. You're lazy. Stupid. You
want motivation? I'll give you some damn motivation—
come here...*

"Julie? Hey, I'm sorry…" Quinn's voice was softer now, edged with regret. She couldn't look at him. She was usually able to control her reactions, but right now she didn't trust herself not to break and either burst into tears or rip into him in a screaming tirade. It had been a long time since she'd done either, but Quinn managed to break through her usual defenses. That realization shook her.

"I've gotta go." She pushed past him, swatting at his hand when he tried to grip her arm. "Don't do that. Just… I need to go. Sorry." She mumbled the last word and kicked herself for it. Apologizing to scolding adults had been her fallback position since she was five. *Sorry, Daddy. Sorry, Mommy. Please don't be mad. Please don't…*

She broke into a near jog toward her car, ignoring Quinn's voice calling after her. He watched in obvious confusion as she drove off. To his credit, he didn't try to stop her. She held herself together until she was off resort property and on the main road, then she cried all the way home. Groceries would have to wait until she could stuff all the ugliness back into the mental vault and pull herself together.

And then she'd have to figure out a way to never, *ever* face Quinn Walker again.

Don't miss
Second-Chance Summer *by Jo McNally,*
available May 2022 wherever
Harlequin Special Edition books and ebooks are sold.

Harlequin.com